THE ROSARY: CHAIN OF HOPE

FATHER BENEDICT J. GROESCHEL, C.F.R.

THE ROSARY
Chain of Hope

IGNATIUS PRESS   SAN FRANCISCO

Cover art: Bartolomeo Esteban Murillo (1618–1682)
Madonna of the Rosary
Palazzo Pitti, Florence, Italy
Photograph by Scala/Art Resource
Cover design by Riz Boncan Marsella

ISBN 0–89870–983–0
Library of Congress Control Number 2003102544
Printed in the United States of America ∞

To Our Blessed Lady,
who is always there for us
in our hours of need

Contents

Acknowledgments

I am deeply grateful to my faithful editor and friend Charles Pendergast for helping me get this little book done in a very short time. The staff at Ignatius Press, especially Tony Ryan and Eva Muntean, have, as always, been most helpful and efficient. May God bless them all.

— Father Benedict J. Groeschel, C.F.R.
Feast of the Annunciation 2003

Art Credits

COVER: Bartolomeo Esteban Murillo (1618–1682), *Madonna of the Rosary*, Palazzo Pitti, Florence, Italy. Photo credit: Scala /Art Resource.

THE JOYFUL MYSTERIES

1. Carl Bloch, *The Annunciation*. Copyright: Frederiksborg Museum, Germany. U.S. Agent: Hope Gallery (www.hopegallery.com).
2. Carl Bloch, *The Visitation*. Copyright: Frederiksborg Museum, Germany. U.S. Agent: Hope Gallery.
3. Carl Bloch, *The Manger Scene*. Copyright: Frederiksborg Museum, Germany. U.S. Agent: Hope Gallery.
4. Simon Vouet (1590–1649), *The Presentation at the Temple*. Louvre, Paris, France. Photo credit: Giraudon/Art Resource, N.Y.
5. Bartolomeo Manfredi (1582–after 1622), *Christ with the Doctors*. Scala, Uffizi, Florence, Italy. Photo credit: Art Resource, N.Y.

THE SORROWFUL MYSTERIES

1. Jacopo Robusti Tintoretto (1518–1594), *Christ in the Garden of Gethsemane*. S. Stefano, Venice, Italy. Photo credit: Cameraphoto/Art Resource, N.Y.
2. Ludovico Carracci (1555–1619), *The Flagellation of Christ*. Musée de la Chartreuse, Douai, France. Photo credit: Giraudon/Art Resource, N.Y.
3. Paolo Caliari, *Christ Mocked*. Veronese, 16th Cenury. © Christie's Images/CORBIS.
4. Caravaggio [Michelangelo Merisi] (1573–1610), *Christ Carrying the Cross*. Kunsthistorisches Museum, Vienna, Austria. Photo credit: Erich Lessing/Art Resource, N.Y.
5. Diego Rodriguez Velazquez (1599–1660), *The Crucifixion*. Museo del Prado, Madrid, Spain. Photo credit: Erich Lessing/Art Resource, N.Y.

THE GLORIOUS MYSTERIES

1. Carl Bloch, *The Resurection*. Copyright: Frederiksborg Museum, Germany. U.S. Agent: Hope Gallery.

2. Jacopo Robusti Tintoretto, *Ascension of Christ* (1579–1580). Scuola Grande di S. Rocco, Italy. Photo credit: Cameraphoto/Art Resource, N.Y.
3. Mirabello Cavalori (c. 1515–after 1572), *Pentecost*. Badia Fiorentina, Florence, Italy. Photo credit: Scala/Art Resource, N.Y.
4. Paolo Veronese (1528–1588), *Assumption of the Virgin*. Musée des Beaux-Arts, Dijon, France. Photo credit: Erich Lessing/Art Resource, N.Y.
5. Diego Rodriguez Velazquez (1599–1660), *The Coronation of the Virgin*. Museo del Prado, Madrid, Spain. Photo credit: Erich Lessing/Art Resource, N.Y.

THE LUMINOUS MYSTERIES

1. Paolo Veronese (1528–1588), *Baptism of Christ*. Palazzo Pitti, Florence, Italy. Photo credit: Scala/Art Resource, N.Y.
2. Palma Giovane (1548–1628), *The Wedding at Cana*. S. Giacomo dell' Orio, Venice, Italy. Photo credit: Cameraphoto/Art Resource, N.Y.
3. Jean-Baptiste de Champaigne (1631–1684), *Sermon on the Mount*. Musée Magnin, Dijon, France. Photo credit: Réunion des Musées Nationaux/Art Resource, N.Y.
4. Raphael (1483–1520), detail from the *Transfiguration*. Pinacoteca, Vatican Museums, Vatican State. Photo credit: Scala/Art Resource, N.Y.
5. Juan de Juanes (1510–1579), *The Last Supper*. Museo del Prado, Madrid, Spain. Photo credit: Scala/Art Resource, N.Y.

CHAPTER ONE

The Rosary in Our Time

In the fall of 2002 the Catholic world, and even the secular media, all expressed a delightful surprise and enthusiasm when Pope John Paul II announced five new mysteries that can be used in the Rosary. The front pages of newspapers, some of them addicted to celebrating the moral failings of a small percentage of the clergy, seemed for a moment to forget their general hostility to the Catholic Church. They printed stories announcing this new document, and evening TV news programs also carried the story. The media attention was somewhat surprising, because the news was of interest principally to devout Catholics, a segment of the population usually ignored by the media. Despite the predictions of some who are hostile to almost all devotion, especially Marian devotion, the Rosary could still command a great deal of attention.

Although many people are devoted to this ancient form of prayer, which is somewhat paralleled by the use of prayer beads in many other religions, the Rosary does not enjoy the universal popularity it had before Vatican II. I recall a sad Friday afternoon in November, nearly forty years ago, when I stood with the entire student body in the quadrangle of a Catholic college as we recited the Rosary for the dead President, shot in Dallas minutes before. I noticed that at least two-thirds of the students, all neatly dressed in suits and ties, had a Rosary in their hands. That was an age when your mother asked you if you had your Rosary in your pocket when you left the house in the morning. Another world.

Yet many people, young and old, are still devoted to the Rosary as a prayer of meditation and thanksgiving. Many will still say the Rosary in time of special need. Pope John Paul II's example and personal devotion to Our Lady and the recitation of the Rosary have encouraged many to pray this prayer.

Why Repetitive Prayer?

Years ago when the Rosary was often mumbled at wakes, our non-Catholic friends and relatives became more and more convinced that Catholicism was indeed a mysterious religion. At times it was almost impossible to understand the Rosary recited in this way. Only for this reason was I relieved when other prayers, more easily understood, were used to remember the dead and commend them to God's merciful love.

Protestants, especially Episcopalians and Presbyterians, were used to beautiful prayers said in beautiful ways. Methodists and Baptists were accustomed to prayers said with lots of soul and feeling. They were all confused by the rapid-fire recitation of the Rosary. They were puzzled not so much that the prayers were largely directed to Christ's Mother, but that this perfunctory monotone recitation would be directed to anyone at all.

Part of the problem for them was that repetitive prayer, which is an ancient practice of almost every world religion, forms no part of Protestantism. Not only prayer beads but also mantras—that is, repeated phrases—and chants are part of much religious practice, the Protestant tradition excepted. How many times did Our Lord Himself repeat the Shema

(Deut 6:4) and other phrases that are part of Jewish worship? He Himself left us a short and most profound prayer that is endlessly repeated by all Christians. In fact, that prayer is part of the Rosary.

The whole idea of repeating prayers and chants is to leave the mind free to ascend to God—to express interiorly feelings, sentiments, and ideas that are almost impossible to put into words, either because the individual does not know the precise theological phrases or, more likely, because the thoughts are so personal that they go beyond verbal expression. It is little recognized that many of the inner events of our psychic lives, especially emotions like joy, sorrow, love, anger, and fear, are not expressed in words, or, if they are, the words are inadequate. When we repeat certain phrases and even actions, like fingering prayer beads, we are invited to prayer and interior recollection, even in very disturbing circumstances.

A personal example might help. My favorite place to say the Rosary is the New York City subway. Entrance into the subway is an apocalyptic event all its own. Picture a dark hole in the earth and endless numbers of apparently dead bodies that stand, sentinel-like, waiting for a train (custom and noise forbid all human interaction in the subway). There is an unearthly screeching of wheels on the rails as well as occasional flashes of electrum when someone drops a potato chip or other organic substances on the tracks. All these beckon the thoughtful soul to think of the four last things, especially purgatory and hell.

In the rhythm of the moving train there is a silence that brings the city dweller to great solitude. I can immerse myself in the mysteries while the beads flow through my hands. Our Franciscan religious habit comes equipped with a very plain wooden Rosary, so I do not even have to be concerned with hiding the beads in my pocket.

If I am too tired or distracted to focus deeply on the mysteries, I switch to intercessory prayer to Our Lady for the many people and intentions that any thoughtful Christian carries in his or her heart. If I should run out of these, I just look around the subway car at my fellow passengers and without much effort see that many of them are burdened, even overwhelmed by life. Some look absolutely desperate. And I let the gentle, beautiful, healing verses of the Our Father and the Hail Mary flow over each of them. As an old Jewish lady once said to me when she received ashes on Ash Wednesday, "It can't hurt, and it's free."

Repetitive prayer can also be healing for the soul. In desperate moments the Rosary can be a lifeline. It has been revealed recently that Mother Teresa lived through decades of deep spiritual darkness. The following words from a letter to her spiritual director are worth memorizing for those times when we can do nothing more than just hold on.

> The other day I can't tell you how bad I felt—there was a moment when I nearly refused to accept—deliberately I took the Rosary and very slowly without even meditating or thinking—I said it slowly and calmly—the moment passed—but the darkness is so dark, and the pain is so painful—but I accept whatever He gives and I give whatever He takes.[1]

So even for Mother Teresa the Rosary was not only an act of devotion but also a place of refuge at certain times amid interior storms of darkness.

Although prayer beads have been known in many cultures for millennia, Catholic prayer beads, or the Rosary, came into existence in the Middle Ages, perhaps through the influence of the Crusaders, who had encountered the use of

[1] From a letter to Father Lawrence T. Picachy, S.J., February 13, 1963.

prayer beads in the East. The fifteenth-century Dominican Blessed Alain de la Roche is credited with popularizing the Rosary to Our Lady. Not long after, a Franciscan Rosary of seven decades became popular. It included the mysteries of the adoration of the Magi and Christ's apparition to His Mother after His Resurrection. However, the Dominican Rosary of fifteen decades was by far the most popular Rosary in the Catholic Church.

The Rosary offers us an opportunity to step back for a few minutes from the noise and din of life, even, as we have seen, from the noise of a subway train. In our busy modern life with its distractions and discouragements, the Rosary can be a wonderful means of prayer and an easy way to come into contact with the presence of God, Our Lady, and the saints. It is an especially good technique for growing in deeper understanding of the Gospel of Jesus Christ. It seems to me that nothing is more important right now than for Christians to become more and more moved by, and filled with, the words of Christ in the Gospels. The mysteries of the Rosary now take us through the whole Gospel, into the mysteries of eternal life, which are dimly but powerfully portrayed in the Book of Revelation.

In order to make this book helpful to those who want to grow in their appreciation of the Rosary, I have chosen the theme of hope. Saint Paul tells us in his epistle to the Romans (8:24) that we are saved by hope, which leads us to patience. And indeed, every Christian looking forward to eternal life after the difficult struggle of this life must be motivated and guided by our blessed hope in Christ Jesus Our Lord. The beautiful virtue of hope is often thought of only when the circumstances of life appear to be hopeless. Then we know that Christian hope goes beyond all human hope. In this set of meditations we will relate the mysteries of Christ to our hope for salvation.

The Mysteries of Christ

The word *mystery* has become associated with each decade
of the Rosary. It is a very beautiful and important term
that has largely lost its meaning in modern times. Mystery
derives from a Greek word meaning "to close one's eyes
and lips". So a mystery is a reality that is present even when
our eyes are closed—that is, when we cannot see or understand it.

As a result of the influence of modernism and skepticism,
the experience of mystery has become less valued in our
culture and even in the Church. The joy of celebrating the
mysteries of God has become almost an embarrassment.
One of the most positive contributions of the new *Catechism
of the Catholic Church* is that it has reintroduced the idea of
mystery into Catholic thinking. Matthias Scheeben, one of
the most influential theologians of the late nineteenth century, reminds us of the importance of mystery in the Christian faith.

> The greater, the more sublime, and the more divine Chris-
> tianity is, the more inexhaustible, inscrutable, unfathomable,
> and mysterious its subject matter must be. If its teaching is
> worthy of the only-begotten Son of God, if the Son of God
> had to descend from the bosom of His Father to initiate us
> into this teaching, could we expect anything else than the
> revelation of the deepest mysteries locked up in God's heart?
> Could we expect anything else than disclosures concerning a
> higher, invisible world, about divine and heavenly things,
> which "eye hath not seen, nor ear heard," and which could
> not enter into the heart of any man (1 Cor. 2:9)? And if God
> has sent us His own Spirit to teach us all truth, the Spirit of
> His truth, who dwells in God and there searches the deep
> things of God (cf. John 16:13; 1 Cor. 2:10 ff), should this
> Spirit reveal nothing new, great, and wondrous, should He
> teach us no sublime secrets? . . .

I would go even further: the truths of Christianity would not stir us as they do, nor would they draw us or hearten us, and they would not be embraced by us with such love and joy, if they contained no mysteries. What makes many a man recoil from the Christian mysteries as from sinister specters is neither the voice of nature nor the inner impulse of the heart nor the yearning for light and truth, but the arrogance of a wanton and overweening pride. When the heart thirsts after truth, when the knowledge of the truth is its purest delight and highest joy, the sublime, the exalted, the extraordinary, the incomprehensible all exercise an especial attraction.[2]

Even in the modern scientific world the greatest of the scientists have often had a strong sense of mystery. Perhaps the most notable of these was Albert Einstein, who consistently enjoyed speaking with Catholic clergy about the mystery of the Holy Eucharist. In a remarkable quotation Einstein said this about mystery:

The fairest thing we can experience is the mysterious. It is the fundamental emotion which stands at the cradle of true art and science. . . . A knowledge of the existence of something we cannot penetrate, of the manifestations of the profoundest reason and the most radiant beauty, which are only accessible to our reason in their most elementary forms—it is this knowledge and this emotion that constitute the truly religious attitude.

The Catholic faith, of course, is filled with mysteries, some of which relate to the life of Christ, the Virgin Birth, and the Resurrection, while others are concerned with those things that Christ has left us to help us on our way to salvation, especially the sacraments (which in the Eastern Church

[2] Matthias Joseph Scheeben, *The Mysteries of Christianity*, as quoted in Benedict J. Groeschel, C.F.R., with Kevin Perrotta, *The Journey toward God* (Ann Arbor, Mich.: Servant Publications, 2000), 68–69.

are referred to as mysteries). Christianity is indeed a religion of mystery. One must have a joy and reverence for the presence of mystery, without which Catholicism would become boring and even repulsive. Attempts to desacralize the sacraments in recent years are rooted in the loss of the sense of mystery. We speak often of the mystery of the Eucharist, but each of the sacraments is a mystery, although none of them is greater than the mystery of faith in the presence of Christ in the Holy Eucharist.

The Rosary in the Twenty-First Century

We live in a time when large numbers of people have lost any sense of mystery, whereas many others harbor a simple peasant's sense of mystery even in our modern world (for example, many of the immigrants to the United States from Africa and Latin America). It is important, therefore, to reaffirm today the mysteries of Christ. Unfortunately, skepticism and rationalism in religious education have undermined the true teaching of the Catholic faith on Christ and his mysteries. Yet this is the core and foundation of our faith. In our meditations on hope, we will return to the central mystery of Christ, and we will look into what is inscrutable. We will try to plumb things that are ultimately unfathomable. And we will kneel in awe and appreciation of the little that we do know through divine revelation of the transcendent mysteries of God.

When non-Catholics in the past used to question the Catholic devotion of the Rosary, I was puzzled. They did not know the mysteries or that we are encouraged to meditate on them as best we can. When they questioned the Rosary, I could hear in my mind the words of Saint Paul: "O the depth of the riches and wisdom and knowledge of God! How unsearchable are his judgments and how inscrutable his ways! 'For who has known the mind of the Lord, or who has been his counselor?'" (Rom 11:33–34).

A Journey to Mystery

In the next fifteen brief mini-chapters and appendix 1, we will try to examine the mysteries, always centering them on the overall encompassing mystery of Christ. You might find this helpful for your reading and meditation if you are preparing to recite one of the series of mysteries. I hope these shared meditations will lead you to many richer ones of your own.

CHAPTER TWO

The Rosary at the Beginning

As we begin the Rosary, it is important to realize that the Church provides us with an introduction. It is a proclamation of faith. This is done in order to remove the Rosary from a mere pious formality or, as it might be in some other religions, simply a matter of recollection and pulling oneself together. The Rosary is not just a ritual or a way of recollection, although it contains aspects of both.

The Creed is an entrance into a garden and a place of faith, and we enter that garden by a proclamation of our absolute faith in God the Father, Jesus Christ, and the Holy Spirit, and in the things that Christ has given us in our faith. The solemn and prayerful recitation of the Creed, therefore, is a very important part of the Rosary. The Lord's Prayer and the three Hail Marys are then added.

People often assign different meanings to these prayers—petitions for faith, hope, and charity, or petitions for the welfare of priests, particularly of Pope John Paul II, who has shown such great interest in the Rosary.

Whatever intentions we may attach to these few prayers, they certainly invite us to quiet meditation and recollection, to step back from life and regroup physically and spiritually, even if we recite the Rosary quietly on the bus or in the subway.

The Doxology, or "Glory Be to the Father . . ."

The mysteries of the Rosary are punctuated by the praise of the Holy Trinity, called the doxology, or the word of glory. This use parallels the recitation of the doxology in the Liturgy of the Hours, in which the Holy Trinity is glorified at the end of every psalm and canticle. Praying this simple but exalted prayer clearly reminds us that we are in God's presence, not in an abstract way, but in the presence of the three Divine Persons. Following the words that Christ spoke about baptism at the end of His earthly ministry, we place ourselves before the eternal mystery of divine love—the three Persons who lovingly relate to each other from all eternity. Thus our meditation and prayer, the work of very limited human minds and hearts, reach up beyond the stars, and we hear the words: "Be still, and know that I am God" (Ps 46:10).

Selecting the Mysteries

We have different sets of mysteries and are free to choose any one that fits our needs on a given day. The traditional assignment of mysteries is: joyful mysteries on Monday and Thursday, sorrowful mysteries on Tuesday and Friday, and glorious mysteries on Wednesday, Saturday, and Sunday.[1] For those who would like to include the luminous mysteries, Pope John Paul II has suggested the glorious mysteries on Sunday, joyful on Monday, sorrowful on Tuesday, glorious on Wednesday, luminous on Thursday, sorrowful on Friday, and joyful on Saturday.[2]

It is interesting to note that when the Holy Father has

---

[1] Traditionally, the joyful mysteries are prayed on the Sundays of Christmastide, the sorrowful mysteries on the Sundays of Lent, etc. The essential point, of course, is prayer, not an arbitrary schedule.

[2] See *Rosarium Virginis Mariae*, no. 30, in appendix 2.

recited the Rosary via international television, he has often mixed different mysteries from different sets, so that in the course of five decades he has included joyful, sorrowful, and glorious mysteries. If you are reciting the Rosary with others, it is no doubt best to observe the accepted days, but if you are praying alone, you can certainly change the established assignment of mysteries to days.

Moving Within

When saying the Rosary, it is important above all to move within, to enter a recollected state. To become recollected is to be set apart from what is going on around us. Many people recite the Rosary as a mantra. This is an ancient practice of repeating a word or phrase, each of which takes up an entire breath. If a person is following this technique in English, two breaths can suffice for the first part the Hail Mary, and two for the second; then two breaths each for the Lord's Prayer and the Glory Be to the Father. This technique gives a rhythm to praying the Rosary and at the same time frees our mind to meditate on the mysteries.

Others prefer to say each prayer of the Rosary as an individual statement to Our Blessed Lady or to the heavenly Father. This approach is particularly popular with younger people, perhaps because the obligation to meditate for a while on a mystery seems a little beyond them. If you are accustomed to recite the Rosary as a mantra, you may find it a bit tedious to use the second technique.

When we try to think of Our Blessed Lady listening to these billions of Hail Marys addressed to her every day, we are puzzled and wonder, How could that be eternal bliss? It would seem that the first method of praying the Rosary— that is, concentrating on the mysteries—is more logical, but I think everyone should do what he finds most helpful. This

method suggests that the Blessed Virgin gives a loving attention to those who pray to her rather than listening to the
innumerable speeches aimed in her direction. An English
spiritual author, Dom John Chapman, once observed that we
should pray as we can and not try to pray as we cannot.

CHAPTER THREE

The Joyful Mysteries

The joyful mysteries are of supreme importance to Catholics at the present time, when the appreciation and acceptance of the mystery of the Incarnation tends to be watered down and rationalized. We need to grow in our understanding and appreciation of the Redemption, which begins with the Incarnation. The Council of Ephesus (A.D. 431) decreed that at a certain moment in time, the eternal Word of God, equal to the Father in all things, left the Father's bosom and took upon Himself a true human body and a true human soul in the womb of the glorious Virgin Mary. That statement is the key to any kind of intelligent Christian appreciation of the Incarnation: God is with us; He is one with us in our earthly existence, one in our flesh and blood. This is a mystery in the most sublime meaning of the word. In this age of rationalistic biblical studies the truth of the Incarnation must be constantly affirmed.

THE FIRST JOYFUL MYSTERY

THE ANNUNCIATION

• *The Annunciation*
Carl Bloch

The events of the Annunciation, as given in the Gospel of Saint Luke, can be known to us only through the testimony of the Virgin Mary herself or by inspiration to the evangelists. No one besides Mary was present at the incredible meeting of the human and divine. This mysterious event described by Saint Luke in a few lines presents a number of the basic foundation stones of Christian belief.

The first and obvious fact of the mystery of the Annunciation is that it is a visitation from a heavenly messenger; something occurs that is completely from outside the natural world. This event can only be an object of faith. It is God's self-revelation in the world. Acceptance of the Annunciation is the foundation of the Christian faith. The second, startling truth is that Mary must give her consent to the invitation given to her. Often in salvation history God has chosen young peasant girls—Ruth in the Old Testament, Joan of Arc, Catherine Labouré, Thérèse of Lisieux, and the children of Fatima. He has chosen these little ones to be his witnesses and instruments for grace in the lives of hundreds of millions of people. In no event is this clearer than in the life of the Virgin Mary. Her consent was necessary, and for this reason from the earliest times she has been called the Mother of the Redeemed, Mother of the Church.

There is no indication that Mary was coerced into accepting God's invitation or that she responded out of some kind of religious intuition. As a humble believing girl from a peasant village, she accepted the word that the Lord had spoken to her. As we meditate on this first mystery, let our hearts be filled with hope in the presence of the Incarnate Word, the Son of God, in the world. He comes to bring salvation to us, to those dear to us, and to as many human beings as possible. This mystery also calls us personally to the response necessary for any true disciple of Christ: We must say Yes to Him. We must give Him our wholehearted consent. We must believe the word that the Lord has spoken.

THE SECOND JOYFUL MYSTERY

ð

THE VISITATION

■ *The Visitation*
  Carl Bloch

In this mystery we move from the sublime and mysterious aspects of the Annunciation to its equally mysterious reality in the world. We move from the transcendent truth of God made man in the Annunciation to a very humble and touchingly human situation. A young girl goes to visit her older cousin who has unexpectedly conceived a child. Both of these women live in humble peasant villages. As we can see from their words, they are both deeply imbued with the truths of the Jewish faith. They are familiar with Scripture. And the beautiful expression of Elizabeth, "And blessed is she who believed that there would be a fulfilment of what was spoken to her from the Lord" (Lk 1:45), fills us with confidence and hope. The great events of salvation, like the Incarnation, come now into the smallest events of human life. The Council of Ephesus proclaimed that it is true to say that God was born, that God suffered, and that God died. The Second Person of the Blessed Trinity, by taking to Himself a human body and human soul, was able to experience human birth and human death. He sanctified all human things. The love and charity of the two cousins present an image that almost every human being can meditate on and receive with warmth. The Lord is coming, but He comes in a humble, gentle, and human way. The mystery of the ages becomes the joy of two humble women of the countryside as they rejoice in each other's pregnancy, as well as in the power of God made manifest in both of them.

THE THIRD JOYFUL MYSTERY

THE NATIVITY

▪ *The Manger Scene*
  Carl Bloch

We have become so familiar with the image of the Nativity of Christ, ranging from great paintings to Christmas decorations, that its incredible reality is somewhat dimmed for us. We think of Christmas lights, family days, good meals, and presents. But the Nativity took place in a dangerous situation among the poorest of the poor. Mary wrapped her newborn baby and placed Him in a manger—an animals' feeding trough. In a very short time He would be a political refugee from the homicidal wrath of an insane ruler. The Incarnation, as seen from God's eyes, was a descent into a turbulent, disobedient, and unredeemed world. The mystery of evil operating in the human race came right to the fore. It is clearly revealed before us in the Nativity, in its poverty, its injustice, and its danger. But at the same time there was tremendous joy. All of creation, on the brink of redemption, rejoiced with the heavenly host, who appeared to announce the great news to humble shepherds, who represent the house of Israel. They heard the message, and they believed; then proceeding "with haste", they decided to "go over to Bethlehem and see this thing that has happened" (Lk 2:15). The Magi—representing the Gentile world—were led by a star to find the Christ. "When they saw the star, they rejoiced exceedingly with great joy." In other words, they believed; and seeing "the child with Mary his mother . . . they fell down and worshiped him" (Mt 2:10–11). In the difficulties of human life we must always affirm our belief in the mysteries of God and the mysteries of Christ. Unfortunately, at the present time, the full impact of the Incarnation has been eroded by skepticism and rationalistic attempts to explain away the mystery in both theology and Scripture scholarship. Kneeling in prayer with the Rosary, however, believers should be unaffected by all of

this and should open their eyes to see this great thing
that has taken place, as the shepherds did in the fields so
long ago.

THE FOURTH JOYFUL MYSTERY

THE PRESENTATION OF CHRIST
IN THE TEMPLE

▪ *The Presentation at the Temple*
 Simon Vouet

The Presentation of the Christ Child in the temple, in fulfillment of the regulations of the Law of Moses, gives us a beautiful example of the humility of the Son of God. He teaches us to obey traditions, laws, and customs. Though He would begin the religion that would end the first covenant and usher in the second covenant, He nonetheless fulfills the requirement of the first covenant, which was, after all, an expression of the divine law. The humble figures of Joseph, Mary, and the Child, who come to make the poor people's offering of two turtledoves, the presence of the elderly Anna and Simeon, both mysterious figures, should banish all skepticism from our minds and help us to appreciate the little things of faith. If you do not know the poor and have had little opportunity to share their religious experience, then this mystery opens up the possibilities of understanding why Christ taught that it is easier for the poor than for the rich to enter the kingdom of heaven. The devout poor are willing to accept humbly and directly, and to fulfill carefully and meticulously, what they know to be the expectations of God.

There is something else to be learned from this event in the temple. It is the value of simple devotion, of humble and heartfelt reverence for God. We live in a time when people evaluate religious acts by "how much we get out of them". In other words, we evaluate them primarily in a psychological way, and this has led to an endless search for ways to make worship more appealing and uplifting.

An experience of the profoundly moving customs of different ethnic groups in the Church, who have their own time-honored traditions, reveals how deeply expressive they can be—the Holy Week processions in the Spanish-speaking world or the carolers in Eastern Europe going with candles and bells to announce the birth of Christ on Christmas Eve.

I remember so well assisting as an altar boy on Sunday mornings long ago when new mothers received a special blessing at the first Mass they attended after the birth of a child. It is true that there is more dialogue and discussion at present in the Church, but there is less of the beauty of simple faith, which we see in Mary and Joseph at the time of the Presentation, when, along with many other couples, they came to fulfill the law and receive a blessing.

THE FIFTH JOYFUL MYSTERY

THE FINDING OF CHRIST IN THE TEMPLE

- *Christ with the Doctors*
  Bartolomeo Manfredi

In so many depictions of the Holy Family there is an unrealistic idealization that can become almost repulsive: beautiful carpenter shops, sunny windows, and the Christ Child dressed in a gold apron helping Joseph at the workbench. While all of this may have an appeal for children, it is not realistic. In the last of the joyful mysteries we confront the incomprehensibility of suffering and the difficulties of human life. Although the finding of the Christ Child is a cause of great joy, the mystery also reflects deep sorrow, fear, and parental concern on the part of Joseph and Mary. It has often been said that God writes straight with crooked lines. This is true even in the life of Jesus Christ. The parents could have been spared the pain of this situation by God's Providence, even by the thoughtfulness of Christ, but they were not. As we meditate on the desperate anxiety of the couple looking for their child, we are reminded that for all of us life has its own mysterious failures, catastrophes, and sorrows. When we are forlorn and anxious, or perhaps deeply grieved, we need to remember that such experiences come not only to us, but they also came to the Messiah and His family.

Anxiety is a familiar component of human life, and perhaps it is more common now in more affluent times. Material comforts and anxiety inexplicably go together. One often encounters in the poor a certain acceptance of life, with its pain and fear. The poor live with an inexplicable hope, born of pain and suffering, that permits them to go on even when disaster has occurred and threatens to strike again.

We all live through anxious moments, and even very dark moments, when our worst fears are realized. Mary and Joseph were relieved to find the Christ Child in the temple. In less than half a lifetime Mary would lose her Son at Calvary in sight of this same temple. This reminds us that Christianity is very much the religion of the God who suffers.

Hope and Joy

As the joyful mysteries come to an end, they present us with hope unbounded—the hope of the Redeemer, the hope of divine adoption, the hope of salvation. They also present us with poignantly human events: Mary's visit to her cousin, the Presentation in the temple, and the finding of the Child. Already the burden of human life—poverty, misunderstandings, human limitations—is obvious in the life of the Messiah. He is the Son of God; He is not a superman. The Bible is the way of truth, not a series of stories like Pollyanna or a set of myths. These events really took place, and they took place in the lives of real people. Our great hope is founded on the fact that one of these very real people was also truly the Son of God and a Divine Person. The message of hope given by the angel—God is with us, Emmanuel—must reach down to all human beings in their own personal lives. In the midst of their greatest difficulties and sorrows, or in the inevitability of age and sickness, they will also have hope because the Son of God has gone before us on the difficult road of humanity, and His Mother has led the way for us.

CHAPTER FOUR

The Sorrowful Mysteries

If you have said the Rosary regularly throughout life, the chances are that your favorite mysteries are the sorrowful ones. They are most meaningful to us in times of grief and trouble, when we are confused, and especially when we experience the loss of dear ones through death. How quickly we turn again to the sorrowful mysteries.

These mysteries sum up the Passion and death of Christ. They do not include all His sorrows; sorrow and suffering were His constant companions during His earthly life. But these are the supreme sorrows of the human race. When the Son of God reaches down to the bottom of the bottom, reaches into every human heart, however corrupt, embraces every black and wicked deed, however sinful, He draws each heart into His Sacred Heart and says, "Father, forgive them, for they know not what they do." Would we have any hope at all if it were not for the sorrowful mysteries of Our Lord Jesus Christ?

Christianity is unique in many ways, and one of its mysterious qualities can be most helpful to us in the sufferings of this life. Christianity, as we said above, is the religion of the God who suffers—human limitation, hunger and fatigue, danger and distress, humiliation and degradation, agony and death. Only a superficial age will overlook the mystery of sorrow in the life of Jesus Christ because superficiality lives on denial: "Let the good times roll." Indeed, there was never a bubble that did not break.

Even the most well-meaning, faithful, and generous people encounter suffering and sorrow. As Blessed Herman of Reichenau, author of the *Salve Regina*, said so well, life is a "valley of tears". The glorious message of the Gospel is that God so loved the world that He sent His beloved Son to walk through this valley to the deepest point of sorrow and to sanctify human suffering by His presence. This profound thought can be a tremendous consolation to the simplest suffering soul. Christ's Cross can be the consolation of any believer facing the mystery of evil and suffering. We do not understand suffering, but we know that God Himself has been with us and has drunk to the dregs the cup of human suffering and sorrow.

THE FIRST SORROWFUL MYSTERY

THE AGONY IN THE GARDEN

- *Christic in the Garden of Gethsemane*
  Jacopo Robusti Tintoretto

The mysterious agony of Christ in the garden would remain as unknowable to us as the Annunciation unless this event had been revealed to the evangelists, or at least revealed to the apostles. It seems unlikely that Christ would have recounted these events during the mysterious forty days He spent on earth after His Resurrection, but perhaps He did. Nevertheless, the words He uttered during His acute agony in the garden are among the most important in the Christian life: "My Father, if it be possible, let this cup pass from me; nevertheless, not as I will, but as you will" (Mt 26:39). All human beings suffer, and many suffer things that are incomprehensible. We are all at least vulnerable to reaching a moment when we say "why?" to God, knowing there is no earthly answer. In cases of the death of young people, terrible injustices, horrible catastrophes, the illness and death of those who are desperately needed—all these and many other circumstances often appear meaningless to those who endure them. We want to ask why, and there is nothing wrong with that, since the Son of God Himself asked, "My God, my God, why have you forsaken me?" (Mt 27:46). Christianity is the religion of the suffering God, and so we see Christ alone in His agony in Gethsemane, no doubt accompanied in prayer by the holy women who are not there, especially His Mother. Abandoned by His sleeping disciples and overwhelmed by sorrow and grief, He nevertheless accepts the cup of humiliation and degradation that will come to Him. We miss much of the point of Christ's Passion if we think only of His physical sufferings on the Cross. It is part of our Christian faith that in those sufferings He also took on Himself the sins of the world. In Saint Paul's words, He took the decree written against us and hung it on the Cross (see Col 2:14). He paid for the sins of the world. The beginning of that payment was the darkness of the garden. And yet it is on that darkness that our hope of eternal life depends.

THE SECOND SORROWFUL MYSTERY

THE SCOURGING AT THE PILLAR

- *The Flagellation of Christ*
  Ludovico Carracci

We move from the silent melancholy and frightening darkness of the garden to the horror of the flagellation: noise and whiplashes, sadism and violence, a concerted effort to make the person suffer all the more.

If the Shroud of Turin is indeed authentic, Christ's body was whipped 110 times. This was almost seventy more lashes than were allowed even in the most brutal torture, because men died of shock under that many whiplashes, and their skin began quickly to deteriorate.

In our easy times when we are afraid of pain, we must reflect on the Messiah's voluntary acceptance of pain during His terrible scourging. Think also of His Mother's pain. Perhaps she was just outside the praetorium and could hear the whiplashes, the yelling and jeering of the soldiers. Think of the pain of the holy women. Think of all the people who have lived with dreadful pain and unanswered questions and who endured inconceivable evils. Yet they knew that the Cross of Christ had triumphed over the worst of human conditions and had given us everlasting hope.

THE THIRD SORROWFUL MYSTERY

THE CROWNING WITH THORNS

- *Christ Mocked*
  Paolo Caliari

The bitter and iniquitous humiliation of the crown of thorns is almost incomprehensible to us. When most Western people think of thorns, we think of rose bushes, whose thorns are bad enough. But the *spinae* of Jerusalem grow three or four inches long. They were made into something like a helmet and pressed down on the skull, ripping the flesh in every direction, perhaps even penetrating parts of the skull where there might have been an anatomical fissure around the edges. How terrible was this pain, how unimaginable! How did Christ even survive such an ordeal? And it was accompanied by mockery—mockery of the Son of God, the King of Kings.

In all our lives we live through unnecessary pain, and we may encounter the mockery of what is very good and very holy. By our own failures we have sometimes even participated in that mockery. The image of the crown of thorns should reach deeply into our souls. In the midst of the bitter sufferings that come to all of us at times, we should have hope because Jesus Christ sanctified suffering and the grief of death and the horror of mental illness. Mother Teresa used to say that mental illness is Jesus' crown of thorns. These words can be an immense consolation and hope to those whose lot it is to wear this crown.

THE FOURTH SORROWFUL MYSTERY

THE CARRYING OF THE CROSS

- *Christ Carrying the Cross*
  Caravaggio

It is almost impossible to comprehend how, after His terrible flagellation and crowning, Jesus of Nazareth was able to carry the Cross along the narrow canyon of the streets known as the Via Dolorosa, with a screaming mob on both sides. Although the soldiers accepted this event as a commonplace form of execution, the Messiah saw in it a warning for the future of Israel and the world. To the wailing women who were following Jesus along the Way of Sorrows, He said, "Do not weep for me, but weep for yourselves and for your children" (Lk 23:28). And these words would indeed be not only a summary of human history before the Passion, but also a prophecy of events to come.

How many human beings have walked for months and years along the path of sorrow? How many people with sickness, tragedy, misunderstanding, humiliation, and their own failures must live through years of pain or imprisonment day after day? The carrying of the Cross through the streets of Jerusalem, this mystery of endurance, of courage and sorrow, should be before the eyes of every thoughtful Christian so that when dark times come, we will remember.

I once visited the Holy Land after a time of great grief and sorrow, the suicide of a youngster with whom I was working. As I came along the Via Dolorosa, I saw the station where Jesus is said to have stopped to speak to His Mother. I knocked on the door, and the Little Sisters of Jesus let me into the chapel that was on the level of the old street—the first Via Dolorosa. There I knelt with my own sorrow and grief and understood that the Messiah had taken on Himself and sanctified all the griefs of human existence.

THE FIFTH SORROWFUL MYSTERY

THE CRUCIFIXION OF
OUR LORD JESUS CHRIST

■ *The Crucifixion*
Diego Rodriguez Velazquez

The crucifixion and death of Jesus are the dramatic end of the narrative of the Passion. Unfortunately, we have seen them depicted only in artistic representations, almost like a tableau. Artists endeavoring to bring out the mystical and spiritual importance of these events have endowed them with a beauty that was not in the original scene. The crucifixion of Jesus was a hideous event. It was vicious, vile, and terribly sadistic torture. Not once in all His Passion did Jesus answer back. Not once did He correct his executioners. In fact, Pilate had to cajole Him into answering simple questions. Jesus did not speak from the Cross to those who mocked Him and told Him to come down. It is said that among the first Christians were people who had mocked Him on that first Good Friday and later repented. May the mockers of today repent, and may we who believe carve the Cross of Jesus on our hearts.

Hope and Suffering

Why did Jesus accept this terrible death? Here the mystery of faith comes together with the mysteries of natural life, the mystery of evil. All world religions seek some answer to the problem of evil. None of the answers is wholly adequate. In Christianity the answer includes the fact that the worst of all evil, the sum of all evils, was taken upon the wounded body of Jesus Christ. He accepted it and forgave the human race for all its sins. He took them away through His obedience and acceptance of the lot of the human being, who was vulnerable and unprotected against the malice of other depraved human beings. Christ was there to accept the worst. And as He accepted the worst, He absolved the sins of the world. "Father, forgive them; for they know not what they do" (Lk 23:34).

CHAPTER FIVE

The Glorious Mysteries

The glorious mysteries, of course, are the ultimate celebration of Christian hope. Throughout the ages, hundreds of millions of people experiencing oppression, grief, sorrow, failure, even slavery, persecution, torture, and death have been consoled by the memory of the Resurrection of Our Lord Jesus Christ. His promise, "I go [to] prepare a place for you . . . that where I am you may be also" (Jn 14:3) is the very answer to why Christianity is the largest of the world religions. How important it is for us to rejoice in the glorious mysteries, which go completely beyond human comprehension. When people lose the sense of mystery, they will not be able to say the Rosary, and they will give it up. On the other hand, those for whom the mysterious promise of eternal life shines brightly will be happy to come to the center of the garden of the Rosary, past the crucifix, and look at the shrine of the empty tomb, at the glorious image of the Redeemer in the center of the garden.

THE FIRST GLORIOUS MYSTERY

THE RESURRECTION

- *The Resurrection*
  Carl Bloch

Along with the Incarnation, the Resurrection of Jesus is the greatest of mysteries ever to take place in this world. The truth of the Resurrection is borne out by the simple fact that the religion of Jesus Christ did not go out of existence, that His work did not end on that terrible Friday afternoon. Rather, His work began that day. And although modern people find it difficult to cope with the idea of the resurrected body, everything in the Gospel—all the testimony of the Gospel writers and others—loudly proclaim that the human body and soul of Jesus were united to His divine being and divine personhood, that it was indeed the same Jesus of Nazareth who spoke to the apostles in the upper room and along the Sea of Galilee.

Many people who have been influenced by skepticism but who are unwilling to give up their belief completely will toy with the idea that the Lord's resurrected body was an apparition. No one familiar with apparitions would think this, because it is recorded that He ate a piece of fish. He asked the apostles to touch His wounds. This is not what is recorded of apparitions. If we look at the best-authenticated and studied apparitions of modern times—those at Lourdes and Fatima—we see that an apparition is totally different from a resurrected body. A resurrected body is just that—a true human body that has come back with a new kind of life, a life that will never end.

It is this Resurrection that gives us the hope of everlasting life. It is the foundation of all Christian worship, belief, and practice. In these skeptical times we should work hard to believe in the Resurrection and manifest our belief to all who are willing to listen. We should explain it as best we can to all who want to know what happens to us when we leave this world.

Martha's words at the time Our Lord raised Lazarus from the dead are so important for us: "I know that he will rise again in the resurrection at the last day." We should repeat them often. We should also frequently repeat Jesus' response to Martha: "I am the resurrection and the life" (Jn 11:24–25).

THE SECOND GLORIOUS MYSTERY

꽃

THE ASCENSION

- *Ascension of Christ*
Jacopo Robusti Tintoretto

The Ascension is a mystery perhaps slightly less startling but just as inscrutable as the Resurrection. Where did Christ go that day when He was lifted up from Mount Olivet and "a cloud took him out of their sight" (Acts 1:9)? Christian painting, based on Scripture, depicts Him disappearing heavenward. But this should not lead us to conclude that His resurrected body is floating around somewhere in space. Saint Mark tells that Christ is very definitely in a particular place, namely, at the Father's right hand.

The account of the Ascension brings us to the edge of physical matter. No scientist would ever be so foolish as to give an explanation of the nature of physical matter, which is one of science's great mysteries. Therefore, any appeal to physics to deny the Resurrection or the Ascension is absurd. We do not know what matter itself is. As believers, we know that Christ passed into another domain of being, but He remained both a human being with his physical body and human soul as well as a Divine Person. Those who are skeptical about this might do well to remember that they will be meeting Him in the fairly near future, when they will come to know what a resurrected body is really like. Perhaps meditation on this mystery may help prepare the skeptics and others to move in that direction even now.

THE THIRD GLORIOUS MYSTERY

THE DESCENT OF THE HOLY SPIRIT
ON THE APOSTLES

• *Pentecost*
Mirabello Cavalori

Devout Christians of all denominations rejoice in the Holy Spirit. We all know from personal experience that He gives us the ability, strength, knowledge, and wisdom to do what is totally beyond our own capacity. The descent of the Holy Spirit is perhaps the most empirically demonstrable truth of the Catholic faith. Over and over we see people doing things, accomplishing things, and overcoming obstacles, even sickness and terminal illness, by the grace of the Holy Spirit. These manifestations should fill us with joy and renewed acceptance of the mysteries of faith.

At a time when the Christian faith is eroded and attacked from without and within, it is important to rely on the Holy Spirit. His gifts, including wisdom, courage, counsel, and reverence, give us a strength beyond any moral fortitude and personal ability. We must invoke the Holy Spirit and rely on Him in order to go on. This will result, as the first Pentecost did, in spiritual gifts for others and unthinkable grace for ourselves.

THE FOURTH GLORIOUS MYSTERY

THE ASSUMPTION OF THE
BLESSED VIRGIN MARY

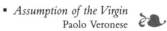

- *Assumption of the Virgin*
  Paolo Veronese

The Assumption of the Blessed Virgin Mary is an extremely important religious event, because it places, alongside the masculine body of the Messiah, the feminine body of His Mother in eternal life. This is a great sign for all of us. Christ returned to eternal life completely by His own power and right. Our Blessed Lady was assumed into heaven, the child of Adam and Eve like the rest of us, though without the effects of original sin; nonetheless, she did not have any more right to everlasting life than the rest of us. But with her Son and Savior, her Child and her God, she precedes us, goes before us. She is our Mother in the next world because she has been our spiritual mother in this world. Unfortunately, not all Catholics have experienced personal assistance through the intercession of the Virgin Mary. Perhaps by good example and prayer we may gather others around us, not only Catholics but non-Catholic Christians as well, to pray for the intercession and help of the Mother of Jesus.

THE FIFTH GLORIOUS MYSTERY

THE CORONATION OF OUR LADY AS
QUEEN OF HEAVEN AND EARTH

- *The Coronation of the Virgin*
  Diego Rodriguez Velazquez

The glorious coronation of Mary, which in no way resembles the coronation of earthly kings and queens, is a mystical event. It is really Mary coming into the glory of the just. We all know, of course, that saints in immense multitudes have joined her already in the kingdom of heaven, awaiting the resurrection of their bodies. But the image of the Mother of Jesus, the humble virgin of Nazareth, Our Lady of Sorrows, the woman at the Cross, now embracing the presence of the most Holy Trinity, should fill all Christians with the greatest hope and reverence for the mystery of eternal life.

As we grow older, we may have a greater share in the sorrows of life and the pains of age. We may experience difficulty and failure and even the betrayal of friends. We may have to accept the reality of dashed hopes, unfulfilled plans, and dreams that can never come to be. As we struggle to accept this suffering, how beautiful and marvelous it is to lift up our eyes and know that with our glorious and risen Savior there is one of His elect, one for whom He is Redeemer, Son, and Lord.

The coronation of the Blessed Virgin Mary, depicted by so many great medieval artists, should encourage and draw each of us to a greater hope of eternal life. For this reason, in the *Divine Comedy*, Dante used the coronation of the Virgin as the introduction and the symbol of the salvation of the just and the mysterious love of the Christ Jesus Our Lord. He wisely took this event to be the end of the journey of the soul.

Hope and Glory

A thousand years ago the severely handicapped Benedictine Blessed Herman of Reichenau (1013–1054), who suffered from palsy, spina bifida, and a cleft palate but was nonetheless a genius, left us a beautiful prayer to summarize the whole goal of the mystery of salvation. That prayer can be said by any Christian in time of darkness or difficulty. Along with the Hail Mary (which is borrowed from Scripture itself), Blessed Herman's prayer sums up the meaning of Christian devotion to the Virgin Mary. At the end of the Rosary we should always say:

> Hail, Holy Queen, Mother of mercy, our life, our sweetness, and our hope. To thee do we cry, poor banished children of Eve. To thee do we send up our sighs, mourning and weeping in this valley of tears. Turn then, most gracious advocate, thine eyes of mercy towards us, and after this our exile, show unto us the blessed fruit of thy womb, Jesus. O clement, O loving, O sweet Virgin Mary.
>
> Pray for us, O Holy Mother of God, that we may be made worthy of the promises of Christ.

Many centuries later the devotion of the Church added the brief invocation after the Hail, Holy Queen. Up until Vatican II it was always said at the end of Mass, along with the prayers for the conversion of Russia.[1] One of these, the prayer to Saint Michael, has made a comeback in some places; the other prayer, for the Church, deserves to be revived in these days of extreme difficulty for the Church everywhere.

> O God, our refuge and our strength, look down with favor upon Thy people who cry to Thee; and through the intercession of the glorious and immaculate Virgin Mary, Mother of God, of her spouse blessed Joseph, of Thy holy apostles Peter and Paul, and all the saints, mercifully and graciously hear the prayers which we pour forth to Thee for the conversion of sinners and for the freedom and exaltation of holy Mother Church. Through the same Christ Our Lord. Amen.

---

[1] Sometimes referred to as the Leonine prayers because they were begun during the time of Pope Leo XIII (1878–1903).

CHAPTER SIX

Prayers for the Mysteries

The following prayers are composed to help you sum up prayerfully what we have written about the Rosary as a message of hope. Each prayer could be used for quiet meditation at the beginning of the decade.

The Annunciation

O Lord Jesus Christ, You come to us in mystery and generosity. Your coming is totally beyond the human mind because You are God, yet You are totally comprehensible to us because You become an infant child. Thy mysteries of heaven and earth come together in this little baby. Give us the grace, O Lord, to kneel in adoration before Your divinity incarnate in this world. Amen.

The Visitation

O Lord Jesus Christ, teach us the humility of Your Mother and the humility that was in Your own life. Humbly, as a gentle country woman, she visits her cousin to do works of kindness and charity. This meeting may seem irrelevant to some and its significance obscure. Yet it is really the beginning of the teaching of Christian charity and love for neighbor. Amen.

The Nativity

O Lord Jesus Christ, help us to kneel at Your Christmas crib, to look at that tiny baby and His tiny skull. Underneath that skull human thoughts are linked to divinity and eternity. This must remain completely incomprehensible to our minds. Lord Jesus, You are mysterious, incomprehensible, and unfathomable, but You are also merciful and caring toward all of us. In the mystery of Your love, O Christ, help us to kneel at the manger, where You were wrapped in humble clothes and surrounded by animals. Amen.

The Presentation of Christ in the Temple

O Lord Jesus Christ, in this mystery You remind us of the humility of Joseph and Mary, of the humility expressed by Your own Divine Person in coming to the temple as one of the poor. Give us the grace to be humble enough to fulfill our religious duties and not try to escape them by rationalizing or pseudo-sophistication. Amen.

The Finding of Christ in the Temple

O Lord Jesus Christ, even Your life and Your coming were fraught with human anxiety and trial. Why should we, as followers of You, expect fewer trials than others? No. We should expect trials, but we should be able to overcome them and carry them with greater ease because we believe in You. Amen.

The Agony in the Garden

Lord Jesus Christ, as eternal Son of God, You chose to enter into the depths of human suffering. All human beings suffer, and You willed to take on that condition in its most bitter form. The mysterious account of Your agony in Gethsemane convinces us that it was Your divine will to identify Yourself entirely with the suffering of humanity. O Lord, help us in our own agonies, in the dark gardens of our life. Strengthen us by the memory of Your example and by the grace You won for us as Your sweat fell to the ground in drops of blood. Amen.

The Scourging at the Pillar

Lord Jesus, our imaginations recoil as we think of this terrible event. Scourging is a barbaric, inhuman act, and You were subject to this cruelty to a degree that makes us wonder how You even survived. We do not dwell on Your scourging often, because it is too painful for us. Yet at times we may go through darkness that would seem as terrible as that scourging. Help us to be courageous in our own suffering and compassionate when we see others being beaten at the pillar of life. Amen.

The Crowning with Thorns

O Lord Jesus, it is almost impossible for us to imagine the intense physical suffering of Your crowning with thorns. This outrageous offense to Your sacred humanity is almost unparalleled in the history of human beings' mistreatment of one another. Why did you allow the soldiers to inflict such a terrible suffering on You? You willingly accepted this barbaric torture because of Your love for us and Your desire for our salvation. At this mystery, Jesus, we also think of the mentally ill, of those whose heads are filled with disturbing, distressing, and destructive thoughts, and we ask You especially to have mercy on them and on us all. Amen.

The Carrying of the Cross

Lord Jesus, the journey from the praetorium to Calvary is not very long, but to a man dying from loss of blood, who has been scourged so fiercely, this journey must seem like a lifetime. Long before, You told those who wished to follow You to take up their cross and carry it. Now, very visibly You do the same thing. For all of us life's journey can be a long Via Dolorosa. We rely on Your example and Your grace to help us carry our cross, and carry it well. Amen.

The Crucifixion

Lord Jesus Christ, our minds stop when we come to the hideous torture You received at the hour of death. On the Cross You take on every form of human suffering. In Your mind, body, and spirit You experience all the pain and desolation that are the result of human sin. The spirituality of the Christian mystics has dwelled on this so often, while the rest of the world finds Your sacrifice incomprehensible. Help us to understand, dear Savior, that You permitted and endured all of this for the salvation of the world. Amen.

The Resurrection

O Lord Jesus Christ, out of the darkness of Calvary comes the brightness of Your glorious return to life by Your own power and in Your own human body. This is the mystery of salvation, the mystery in which we hope for our eternal life.

The human mind cannot believe without the gift of faith and cannot rejoice without the presence of the Holy Spirit. Strengthen us to believe in You and trust in Your word. Lift up our hearts when we contemplate this beautiful mystery of the Resurrection that we may be guided through life's difficulties and challenges by the light of the Holy Spirit. Amen.

The Ascension

O Lord Jesus, You leave us this mysterious event to make clear the hope of eternal life. You might simply have disappeared from this world after the work of the forty days, but You did not. You leave us with the image of Your rising into the heavens, but You went far beyond any cosmic heaven. You moved into another domain of being, into the place of eternal life and endless day. In the sorrows of death and loss keep before our eyes the shining mystery of the Ascension. Amen.

The Descent of the Holy Spirit on the Apostles

O Lord Jesus, You explicitly say that You left the world in order to send us the Holy Spirit. This word is so mysterious to us because the Holy Spirit was already present in so many ways. You give us the fullness of the Holy Spirit in Your Gospel, in Your own message of salvation, and in the Church You established through Your apostles and in Your promises to them. Help us to rely on the Holy Spirit so that in our journey through life we may desire the things of heaven and not be tempted by the things of earth. Grant that through the power and gifts of Your Holy Spirit we may go far beyond what we could otherwise accomplish. Amen.

The Assumption of the Blessed Virgin Mary

O Lord Jesus Christ, You have given believers the beautiful vision of the Assumption of Our Lady. Christians have believed that Your Mother followed You body and soul on that unthinkable and impenetrable journey into the next world. When death robs us, when we are frustrated or despondent because of the loss of those whom we loved and relied on, help us to keep before our eyes the promise You gave in Your Mother's Assumption, body and soul, into eternal life. We cannot raise ourselves as human beings, but like Mary, we may hope that we will be taken up from this changing world into one that goes completely beyond human nature and human expectations. Amen.

The Coronation of Our Lady as Queen of Heaven and Earth

Lord Jesus, Your Church gives us this beautiful image based on the final book of Your divine word. The coronation of Your Mother is the glory of all the saints. She leads the saved, Your people, into the everlasting life that cannot be taken away or changed. The vision of Our Lady in glory goes beyond our mental limitations, but not beyond the limits of our hearts. Give us the grace always to lift up our hearts and minds to this hope. Help us to be guided in our daily struggles by the light of the world to come, where You and Your Mother await us as King and Queen of creation and where, with the Father and the Holy Spirit, You are our eternal destiny. Amen.

Epilogue

It is a good idea to keep a Rosary with you. Let it become your companion. This little tangible religious article attached to a crucifix reminds you of your heavenly hope, of what the Son of God had to do and endure that you might have that hope. Let the Rosary open up your heart and mind, even when you finger it as an expression of the hope of eternal life.

Sometimes I see poor children who are hardly instructed at all wearing a Rosary around their necks. Some will say, "Oh, that's not proper." I never correct them. In fact, I have given out thousands of Rosaries to the poor. They could do a lot worse than have a Rosary around their necks. Although they have so little in this world, they have this sign, which has been reinforced by mystical visions at Lourdes and Fatima. The Rosary represents the Blessed Virgin's power of protection for those who ask her intercession with God. It is important to remember that at the Lourdes and Fatima apparitions, approved by the Church, Our Lady was holding the Rosary. That should be enough for any faithful believer.

The Oldest Prayer to Mary

The oldest known prayer to the Virgin Mary is believed to have come from the time of the persecutions of Septimius Severus (193–211) and Decius (249–251). Shortly after that, a chapel was built in Egypt by Patriarch Theonas of Alexandria and named the Church of Saint Mary the Virgin Mother of God. From the Ethiopian, or Coptic, rite we obtain this prayer, which may have been said as early as the end of the second century:

> We fly to thy protection, O Holy Mother of God. Do not ignore our supplications in our trials, but deliver us from many dangers, O pure and blessed one.

Of course the first part of the Hail Mary is older than this prayer because it comes directly from Saint Luke's Gospel. But it was woven into a prayer only a little after the prayer "We fly to thy protection." [1] It would be very wise for all Catholic Christians in this time of crisis in the Church to fly to the protection of the Virgin Mary. The Holy Father has called on us to do this in the year of the Rosary. He himself has been the Pontiff of hope. He has written extensively about hope, and those of us who are accustomed to pray for the intercession of the Blessed Virgin Mary know that she, as the Mother of our Savior, is our life, our sweetness, and our hope.

---

[1] Often referred to by its original title, the "Sub tuum praesidium".

APPENDIX ONE

The Luminous Mysteries

When the Holy Father suggested meditations upon five mysteries from the public life of Our Lord Jesus Christ, not only did this take the Catholic world by surprise, but, as we mentioned, it also generated a good deal of interest in the secular press. This is because the Rosary is such an obvious part of Catholic life. Unfortunately, not as obvious as it used to be.

When the Rosary was first composed, the goal was to include 150 Aves to represent the 150 psalms in the Psalter. Even during the Church's first millennium a string of 150 beads, known as Pater Noster beads, were used to say the Lord's Prayer in place of 150 psalms. By the ninth century, beads were in use among the non-reading lay brothers and sisters of religious communities, and by the eleventh century they were popular with the laity. Then the prayers changed from the Lord's Prayer to the Hail Mary because there was a "Little Office of the Blessed Virgin Mary", and groups of people such as those we have mentioned were saying the Rosary in place of the Office. Those who could not say the Office of the Church, built around the psalms, could at least say the Rosary. By including the principal mysteries of Christ's public life, the Holy Father draws our attention to the whole mysterious ministry of Christ, on which the Christian life of the future would be based. The new mysteries especially relate to the sacraments, which are not explicit in the other mysteries. The five new mysteries—the Baptism of Christ, the Marriage Feast of Cana, the Proclamation of the Kingdom, the Transfiguration, and the Establishment of the Holy Eucharist—are among the most important events in the public life of Our Lord Jesus Christ. Each of the events has many messages and truths for us to contemplate for a more profound understanding of what Our Savior did for the human race in the three brief years of his public life.

Many of us are convinced that the much-needed reform of the Church in these troubled times will require a return to the meditation on the Gospels, which are the very foundation of Christianity. Even the other New Testament books can be seen as commentaries on the Gospels. What the Torah is to the Jews, the Gospels are to Christians. If you are looking for a way to be part of the reform movement that the Church so desperately needs at this time, I could advise you to do nothing better than meditate on the Rosary and particularly on the events of Christ's life as they are presented in the luminous mysteries.

THE FIRST LUMINOUS MYSTERY

THE BAPTISM OF OUR LORD JESUS CHRIST

- *Baptism of Christ*
  Paolo Veronese

In an astonishing and unpredictable event, Jesus Christ, the Messiah, presents Himself to his cousin John to receive the baptism of repentance. John's baptism was not the baptism of salvation and redemption, but it was a baptism of repentance and hope. The ritual of baptism, or spiritual purification through the sign of water, was known not only among the Jews, but among many other ancient people. John, therefore, was not doing something new. That Jesus should come up and humble Himself to receive John's baptism reveals the extent to which the Messiah was willing to go to obtain salvation for the world. This is a glorious proclamation of His humanity, a sense of which has at times been obscured as people focused almost exclusively on His divinity. Although Christ's humanity is not denied at the present time, we need to meditate on this truth, for he calls us, His brothers and sisters of the human race, to repentance. He Himself has no need of repentance, but He shows us the way by receiving John's baptism. He fulfills all justice. If the sign of repentance is part of the life of the Messiah, how can any Christian hesitate when called to examine his conscience and repent of sins and shortcomings?

In choosing the baptism as the first luminous mystery, the Holy Father has also indicated his hope for repentance on the part of every Christian. So many young people of our time have been so badly damaged and scarred by the immorality in which they live and the bad teachings to which they are exposed that they may be afraid of repentance, and yet they need it perhaps more than anyone else. They are not more guilty than others, because they have been deceived and neglected, but they feel more guilty because they have perhaps committed more and darker acts of sin.

Consider the magnificent and mysterious image of Jesus of

Nazareth kneeling in the muddy waters of the Jordan next to the astonished prophet dressed in camel hair. This picture should be written on the minds of everyone so that we will make repentance and confession of sin an important part of our spiritual lives. Repentance for a sinner is the key to the door of hope, hope for divine mercy, hope for eternal salvation.

THE SECOND LUMINOUS MYSTERY

❧

THE MARRIAGE FEAST OF CANA

▪ *The Wedding at Cana*
  Palma Giovane

The Holy Father selected the mysterious marriage feast where Jesus first shows His glory to His disciples as the second point of meditation for Christians in Christ's public life. This marriage feast has often been the subject of rather elaborate paintings and stained-glass windows. Actually it would have been a rather plain affair of peasant people in the tiny village that was just down the road from Nazareth. To this day the town of Cana does not amount to a great deal.

The style of the marriage feast would have included customs not familiar to us—for example, men and women would have been seated on opposite sides of the room. But there would have been music and dancing—men with men and women with women. There would also have been toasting and obviously the drinking of wine and other forms of celebration. Along with this, in true Jewish style, the wedding promises and prayers would have taken place at the reception. So it was both a religious and a social event.

Remember that at this time Our Lord was only beginning to be known as a preacher, as He went through the towns and villages calling people to repentance and healing the sick. Some of His followers or disciples were with Him at the wedding in Cana, but as yet He had not shown His miraculous power to any of them. This "first of his signs" (Jn 2:11) by which He manifested His glory was given at a humble peasant wedding with a miracle that is almost funny. He changes the water into wine. Modern skepticism, of course, has trouble with this, but what an unhappy thing modern skepticism is, anyway. The skeptics would not have drunk the wine even if they had been there. Poor things.

The marriage feast of Cana is not only a sign of Christ beginning to manifest Himself to the world—part of the

Epiphany—but it is also the beginning of the revelation of the Holy Eucharist. The astonishing transformation of the substance of water into the substance of wine (which has been called water *in excelsis*) is meant to prepare human minds for the changing of bread and wine into the body and blood of Christ. It is a miracle. Either you believe it, or you do not believe it. And as Albert Einstein once said, there are only two kinds of people—those for whom everything is a miracle and those for whom nothing is a miracle.

We who are fervent followers of Christ must believe in miracles. If God could make the world, He could certainly change the substance of water into wine, just as He changes the substance of bread each day into the body of Christ. Do not miss the profound theological aspects of this miracle. It is a sign of hope given to the world: Christ will come down into our everyday life; He will bless the marriage; He will bless the meal; He will even bless the party; and He will be there with us and for us.

When I was a child, my great-aunt taught us a beautiful old German grace: "Lord Jesus Christ, be Thou our guest, and share the food that Thou hast blest." The prayer, which is still said in German-speaking lands, reminded us that Jesus was at the table with us, that even in the simplest events of daily life the divine presence is there. If you have ever been to the Passover with the Jews, you will know that there is a recognition of the divine presence at the table. We Christians can hardly do less when the divine presence is with us under the appearance of bread and wine and when our Master has come humbly to bless the bride and groom and be part of their joy. This is our hope: God loves us even in little things.

THE THIRD LUMINOUS MYSTERY

❧

THE PROCLAMATION OF THE KINGDOM

▪ *Sermon on the Mount*
Jean–Baptiste de Champaigne

Certainly the Holy Father was looking for a mystery that would encompass the innumerable, fascinating, and utterly necessary events of Christ's life. You could perhaps make five hundred mysteries of the Rosary if you wanted to single out each parable, each miracle, each event, and each topic within the Sermon on the Mount. But the Holy Father comprehensively places them together in the preaching of the kingdom.

How many times have we seen beautiful paintings of Jesus preaching on the roads of Galilee, or perhaps in the streets of Jerusalem, or by the temple? Unfortunately, because of the skepticism that has entered Christian life, we do not pay enough attention to His preaching. Many people are not familiar with what Christ said, while others use His words solely for polemical arguments. The best place to read the teachings of Christ in the Gospel is on your knees in prayer. May I suggest that if you have never done so, you take one of the Gospels as soon as possible, carve out a period of time when you will not be disturbed, and read the entire Gospel in one sitting or kneeling. The overall impact, I guarantee, will be astonishing.

We are all aware that the preaching of the kingdom of God is minimized in our time by the folly and slander of the media, which have become the vipers' tangle of modern times. The great antidote to this poison is to read the words of the Messiah Himself. As we meditate on this mystery of the preaching of the kingdom, we ought to take one sentence, one word: "How blessed are the poor in spirit" (Mt 5:3) . . . "Sufficient for the day is the evil thereof" (Mt 6:34) . . . "Come to me, all who labor and are heavy laden" (Mt 11:28). These are just a few of the short phrases I memorized as a teenager. They come back to me even now. As you meditate on this mystery, be sure that your mind is focused on the preaching of the kingdom. No one knew that preaching better, no one was more attentive to it, than the Mother of Jesus.

THE FOURTH LUMINOUS MYSTERY

THE TRANSFIGURATION
OF THE LORD

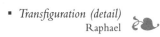
Transfiguration (detail)
Raphael

Unfortunately, our lack of the sense of mystery has caused us to pay less attention to the mystery of the Transfiguration than we ought to. In this mysterious event (properly called a theophany, or a manifestation of the divine presence in the material world), the divinity of Christ is clearly shown to the three disciples and the Resurrection is foretold.

When speaking to a distinguished Scripture scholar a few years ago, I told him how one preacher had reduced this marvelous event to the apostles seeing the glinting of the sun on the snow on Mount Tabor and merely thinking that Christ was transfigured. What nonsense! The scholar, who was deeply appalled when I told him of this preaching, said to me, "Don't you know that's the most succinct and eloquent description of a mystical event in the literature of the world." I said, "Oh, yes, I know, but some of the people who are teaching the Bible right now don't seem to know it."

This marvelous incomprehensible mystery is unprovable at this stage by any means, and it was probably unprovable at the very time that it happened, except to the three witnesses. This Transfiguration shows us the mystery of faith and hope. We all hope to see the transfigured Christ at the end of our lives. We hope to go into eternal life with Him. Let us join Our Blessed Lady, who gave birth to the body that would be transfigured, to the face that would shine like the sun. Let us join her in adoration of the mysterious Messiah, who alone is our hope.

THE FIFTH LUMINOUS MYSTERY

❦

THE INSTITUTION OF THE
HOLY EUCHARIST

▪ *The Last Supper*
  Juan de Juanes

From the earliest days of the Church, following Saint Paul, Christian worship has been related to the Eucharist, to the blessing of bread and wine that became Christ's true body and blood. We find this in the earliest apostolic fathers—Saint Clement, the fourth bishop of Rome; Saint Ignatius, bishop of Antioch; and Saint Justin Martyr. Unfortunately, the adoration and reverence due to the Eucharist have been seriously eroded today as a result of skepticism. Nothing would restore Catholic life more strongly and pointedly than a return to true veneration and custody of the Holy Eucharist and the deeply reverent celebration of Mass. If you think I am exaggerating, ask yourself: How many who receive Holy Communion hardly know what they are doing?

By including the establishment of the Holy Eucharist as a mystery that can be used in the Rosary, the Holy Father calls us to pray for a renewed faith in the Eucharist and renewed zeal and reverence for the meaning of this mystery. How important it is for each of us to bend in silent adoration before the hidden Godhead in the Eucharist. On the night of the Last Supper, so weighted with meaning and sorrow, the apostles were filled with awe and did not know what was happening. To this very day and to the end of the world, believing Christians will be filled with awe and will not be able to understand completely what is happening, because the Eucharist is the mystery of faith. To the struggling soul, to the converting sinner, to the penitent person, even to the spiritually advanced person, the Holy Eucharist is the bread of hope and the promise of eternal life.

Hope and the Luminous Mysteries

"Lord, to whom shall we go? You have the words of eternal life" (Jn 6:68). Saint Thomas Aquinas, writing of the Holy

Eucharist, reminds us that nothing can be truer than the words of Truth Himself. Perhaps other times have been as foolish as our own; perhaps they have questioned Christ, His teaching, His truth, and His holy life and death. But in this vainglorious and silly time, more indirectly than directly, we find that even those who style themselves Christians can be questioning Christ's proclamation of the kingdom.

They present us with a "crippled Christ", who does not know His own identity, purpose, or destiny. He does not know what He is doing or why He is doing it. It is enough to make angels weep and devils laugh. The following remarkable expression of faith from Saint Augustine's *Confessions* sums up the luminous mysteries, those enlightened by the light of endless day that burned in the soul of Our Savior. Augustine compares the creation of the world with the creation of the Church by Christ and the Holy Spirit.

> Proceed in Your confession, O my faith; say to your Lord God: Holy, Holy, Holy, O Lord my God: in Your name were we baptized, O Father, Son, and Holy Ghost, in your name do we baptize, O Father, Son, and Holy Ghost. For among us also God has in his Christ created a *heaven and earth*, the spiritual and carnal members of His Church. And our "earth," before it received the form of doctrine, was *invisible and formless*, and wrapped in the darkness of ignorance, for *Thou hast corrected man for iniquity* and *Thy judgments are a great deep.*
>
> But because your Spirit moved over the waters, Your mercy did not abandon our wretchedness; and You said: *Be light made; Do penance, for the Kingdom of God is at hand. Do penance; be light made.*[1]

[1] Augustine, *Confessions*, XIII, xii, trans. Frank Sheed (New York: Sheed & Ward, 1943), 328–29.

PRAYERS FOR THE LUMINOUS MYSTERIES

The Baptism of Our Lord Jesus Christ

O Lord Jesus Christ, in Your great humility You kneel with sinners and ask to undergo the ritual baptism, the symbolic washing away of sins. You who have no sin, teach us to be subject to the prescriptions, not of the old Jewish law but of the Church, of the new Jerusalem. Give us the grace never to exempt ourselves from these spiritual and psychological actions, which are of such benefit to our personal spiritual life. Amen.

The Marriage Feast of Cana

How humble You are, O Jesus, to go to this little country reception, and how compassionate and light-hearted. You will even work Your first miracle so that a young bride and groom may not be embarrassed at their own wedding. Teach us, O Lord, to be considerate and gentle and to try to bring some joy to those who have very little. Amen.

The Proclamation of the Kingdom

O Lord Jesus Christ, teach us to accept Your holy words, Your counsels, Your commandments, and Your preaching of the road that leads to Your kingdom. How often we become distracted by our own thoughts or the rationalizings of others. Give us the grace to sit quietly and read Your word, meditate on Your Gospel, and hear Your voice. Grant that we may truly know what we must do to enter the kingdom of heaven. Amen.

The Transfiguration of the Lord

O Lord Jesus Christ, give us the grace to believe in Your mysteries, and grant that we may never try to explain them away or pretend that they did not happen. We pray on our knees in the presence of You, our transfigured Lord, remembered in Holy Scripture. We ask to be included in that small group of apostles who saw Your glory and who believed in You. Amen.

The Institution of the Holy Eucharist

O Lord Jesus Christ, so long ago You gave Yourself as the living bread come down from heaven. You proclaimed Your sacrament in words and parables, especially at the celebration of the Last Supper. Each day You ask us to respond to You with reverence and love. Give us the grace to do this. Amen.

Apostolic Letter
Rosarium Virginis Mariae
of the Supreme Pontiff John Paul II
to the Bishops, Clergy and Faithful
on the Most Holy Rosary

INTRODUCTION

1. The Rosary of the Virgin Mary, which gradually took form in the second millennium under the guidance of the Spirit of God, is a prayer loved by countless Saints and encouraged by the Magisterium. Simple yet profound, it still remains, at the dawn of this third millennium, a prayer of great significance, destined to bring forth a harvest of holiness. It blends easily into the spiritual journey of the Christian life, which, after two thousand years, has lost none of the freshness of its beginnings and feels drawn by the Spirit of God to "set out into the deep" (*duc in altum!*) in order once more to proclaim, and even cry out, before the world that Jesus Christ is Lord and Savior, "the way, and the truth and the life" (Jn 14:6), "the goal of human history and the point on which the desires of history and civilization turn".[1]

The Rosary, though clearly Marian in character, is at heart a Christocentric prayer. In the sobriety of its elements, it has

---

[1] Pastoral Constitution on the Church in the Modern World *Gaudium et Spes*, 45.

all the *depth of the Gospel message in its entirety*, of which it can be said to be a compendium.[2] It is an echo of the prayer of Mary, her perennial *Magnificat* for the work of the redemptive Incarnation which began in her virginal womb. With the Rosary, the Christian people *sits at the school of Mary* and is led to contemplate the beauty on the face of Christ and to experience the depths of his love. Through the Rosary the faithful receive abundant grace, as though from the very hands of the Mother of the Redeemer.

The Popes and the Rosary

2. Numerous predecessors of mine attributed great importance to this prayer. Worthy of special note in this regard is Pope Leo XIII who on September 1, 1883, promulgated the Encyclical *Supremi Apostolatus Officio*,[3] a document of great worth, the first of his many statements about this prayer, in which he proposed the Rosary as an effective spiritual weapon against the evils afflicting society. Among the more recent Popes who, from the time of the Second Vatican Council, have distinguished themselves in promoting the Rosary I would mention Blessed John XXIII[4] and above all Pope Paul VI, who in his Apostolic Exhortation *Marialis Cultus* emphasized, in the spirit of the Second Vatican Council, the Rosary's evangelical character and its Christocentric inspiration. I myself have often encouraged the frequent recitation of the Rosary. From my youthful years this prayer has held an important place in my spiritual life. I was powerfully reminded of this during my recent visit to Poland, and in

---

[2] Pope Paul VI, Apostolic Exhortation *Marialis Cultus* (February 2, 1974), 42: AAS 66 (1974), 153.

[3] Cf. *Acta Leonis XIII*, 3 (1884), 280–89.

[4] Particularly worthy of note is his Apostolic Epistle on the Rosary *Il religioso convegno* (September 29, 1961): AAS 53 (1961), 641–47.

particular at the Shrine of Kalwaria. The Rosary has accompanied me in moments of joy and in moments of difficulty. To it I have entrusted any number of concerns; in it I have always found comfort. Twenty-four years ago, on October 29, 1978, scarcely two weeks after my election to the See of Peter, I frankly admitted: "The Rosary is my favorite prayer. A marvelous prayer! Marvelous in its simplicity and its depth. . . . It can be said that the Rosary is, in some sense, a prayer-commentary on the final chapter of the Vatican II Constitution *Lumen Gentium*, a chapter which discusses the wondrous presence of the Mother of God in the mystery of Christ and the Church. Against the background of the words *Ave Maria* the principal events of the life of Jesus Christ pass before the eyes of the soul. They take shape in the complete series of the joyful, sorrowful and glorious mysteries, and they put us in living communion with Jesus through—we might say—the heart of his Mother. At the same time our heart can embrace in the decades of the Rosary all the events that make up the lives of individuals, families, nations, the Church, and all mankind. Our personal concerns and those of our neighbor, especially those who are closest to us, who are dearest to us. Thus the simple prayer of the Rosary marks the rhythm of human life."[5]

With these words, dear brothers and sisters, I set *the first year of my Pontificate* within the daily rhythm of the Rosary. Today, *as I begin the twenty-fifth year of my service as the Successor of Peter*, I wish to do the same. How many graces have I received in these years from the Blessed Virgin through the Rosary: *Magnificat anima mea Dominum!* I wish to lift up my thanks to the Lord in the words of his Most Holy Mother, under whose protection I have placed my Petrine ministry: *Totus Tuus!*

---

[5] Angelus: *Insegnamenti di Giovanni Paolo II*, I (1978): 75–76.

October 2002—October 2003: The Year of the Rosary

3. Therefore, in continuity with my reflection in the Apostolic Letter *Novo Millennio Ineunte*, in which, after the experience of the Jubilee, I invited the people of God to "start afresh from Christ",[6] I have felt drawn to offer a reflection on the Rosary, as a kind of Marian complement to that Letter and an exhortation to contemplate the face of Christ in union with, and at the school of, his Most Holy Mother. To recite the Rosary is nothing other than *to contemplate with Mary the face of Christ*. As a way of highlighting this invitation, prompted by the forthcoming 120th anniversary of the aforementioned Encyclical of Leo XIII, I desire that during the course of this year the Rosary should be especially emphasized and promoted in the various Christian communities. I therefore proclaim the year from October 2002 to October 2003 *the Year of the Rosary*.

I leave this pastoral proposal to the initiative of each ecclesial community. It is not my intention to encumber but rather to complete and consolidate pastoral programs of the Particular Churches. I am confident that the proposal will find a ready and generous reception. The Rosary, reclaimed in its full meaning, goes to the very heart of Christian life; it offers a familiar yet fruitful spiritual and educational opportunity for personal contemplation, the formation of the People of God, and the new evangelization. I am pleased to reaffirm this also in the joyful remembrance of another anniversary: the fortieth anniversary of the opening of the Second Vatican Ecumenical Council on October 11, 1962, the "great grace" disposed by the Spirit of God for the Church in our time.[7]

---

[6] AAS 93 (2001), 285.

[7] During the years of preparation for the Council, Pope John XXIII did not fail to encourage the Christian community to recite the Rosary for the success of this ecclesial event: cf. Letter to the Cardinal Vicar (September 28, 1960): AAS 52 (1960), 814–16.

Objections to the Rosary

4. The timeliness of this proposal is evident from a number of considerations. First, the urgent need to counter a certain crisis of the Rosary, which in the present historical and theological context can risk being wrongly devalued, and therefore no longer taught to the younger generation. There are some who think that the centrality of the Liturgy, rightly stressed by the Second Vatican Ecumenical Council, necessarily entails giving lesser importance to the Rosary. Yet, as Pope Paul VI made clear, not only does this prayer not conflict with the Liturgy, *it sustains it*, since it serves as an excellent introduction and a faithful echo of the Liturgy, enabling people to participate fully and interiorly in it and to reap its fruits in their daily lives.

Perhaps too, there are some who fear that the Rosary is somehow unecumenical because of its distinctly Marian character. Yet the Rosary clearly belongs to the kind of veneration of the Mother of God described by the Council: a devotion directed to the Christological center of the Christian faith, in such a way that "when the Mother is honored, the Son . . . is duly known, loved and glorified".[8] If properly revitalized, the Rosary is an aid and certainly not a hindrance to ecumenism!

A Path of Contemplation

5. But the most important reason for strongly encouraging the practice of the Rosary is that it represents a most effective means of fostering among the faithful that *commitment to the contemplation of the Christian mystery* which I have proposed in the Apostolic Letter *Novo Millennio Ineunte* as a genuine "training in holiness": "What is needed is a Christian life

[8] Dogmatic Constitution on the Church *Lumen Gentium*, 66.

distinguished above all in the *art of prayer*." [9] Inasmuch as contemporary culture, even amid so many indications to the contrary, has witnessed the flowering of a new call for spirituality, due also to the influence of other religions, it is more urgent than ever that our Christian communities should become "genuine schools of prayer".[10]

The Rosary belongs among the finest and most praiseworthy traditions of Christian contemplation. Developed in the West, it is a typically meditative prayer, corresponding in some way to the "prayer of the heart" or "Jesus prayer" which took root in the soil of the Christian East.

Prayer for Peace and for the Family

6. A number of historical circumstances also make a revival of the Rosary quite timely. First of all, the need to implore from God *the gift of peace*. The Rosary has many times been proposed by my predecessors and myself as a prayer for peace. At the start of a millennium which began with the terrifying attacks of September 11, 2001, a millennium which witnesses every day in numerous parts of the world fresh scenes of bloodshed and violence, to rediscover the Rosary means to immerse oneself in contemplation of the mystery of Christ who "is our peace", since he made "the two of us one, and broke down the dividing wall of hostility" (Eph 2:14). Consequently, one cannot recite the Rosary without feeling caught up in a clear commitment to advancing peace, especially in the land of Jesus, still so sorely afflicted and so close to the heart of every Christian.

A similar need for commitment and prayer arises in relation to another critical contemporary issue: *the family*, the primary cell of society, increasingly menaced by forces of

[9] No. 32: AAS 93 (2001), 288.
[10] Ibid., 33: loc. cit., 289.

disintegration on both the ideological and practical planes, so as to make us fear for the future of this fundamental and indispensable institution and, with it, for the future of society as a whole. The revival of the Rosary in Christian families, within the context of a broader pastoral ministry to the family, will be an effective aid to countering the devastating effects of this crisis typical of our age.

"Behold, Your Mother!" (Jn 19:27)

7. Many signs indicate that still today the Blessed Virgin desires to exercise through this same prayer that maternal concern to which the dying Redeemer entrusted, in the person of the beloved disciple, all the sons and daughters of the Church: "Woman, behold your son!" (Jn 19:26). Well-known are the occasions in the nineteenth and the twentieth centuries on which the Mother of Christ made her presence felt and her voice heard, in order to exhort the People of God to this form of contemplative prayer. I would mention in particular, on account of their great influence on the lives of Christians and the authoritative recognition they have received from the Church, the apparitions of Lourdes and of Fatima;[11] these shrines continue to be visited by great numbers of pilgrims seeking comfort and hope.

Following the Witnesses

8. It would be impossible to name all the many Saints who discovered in the Rosary a genuine path to growth in holiness. We need but mention Saint Louis Marie Grignion de

---

[11] It is well-known and bears repeating that private revelations are not the same as public revelation, which is binding on the whole Church. It is the task of the Magisterium to discern and recognize the authenticity and value of private revelations for the piety of the faithful.

Montfort, the author of an excellent work on the Rosary,[12] and, closer to ourselves, Padre Pio of Pietrelcina, whom I recently had the joy of canonizing. As a true apostle of the Rosary, Blessed Bartolo Longo had a special charism. His path to holiness rested on an inspiration heard in the depths of his heart: "Whoever spreads the Rosary is saved!"[13] As a result, he felt called to build a Church dedicated to Our Lady of the Holy Rosary in Pompei, against the background of the ruins of the ancient city, which scarcely heard the proclamation of Christ before being buried in A.D. 79 during an eruption of Mount Vesuvius, only to emerge centuries later from its ashes as a witness to the lights and shadows of classical civilization. By his whole life's work and especially by the practice of the "Fifteen Saturdays", Bartolo Longo promoted the Christocentric and contemplative heart of the Rosary and received great encouragement and support from Leo XIII, the "Pope of the Rosary".

CHAPTER I

CONTEMPLATING CHRIST WITH MARY

A Face Radiant as the Sun

9. "And he was transfigured before them, and his face shone like the sun" (Mt 17:2). The Gospel scene of Christ's Transfiguration, in which the three Apostles Peter, James and John appear entranced by the beauty of the Redeemer, can be seen as *an icon of Christian contemplation*. To look upon the face of Christ, to recognize its mystery amid the daily events and the sufferings of his human life, and then to grasp the divine splendor definitively revealed in the Risen Lord,

---

[12] *The Secret of the Rosary.*

[13] Blessed Bartolo Longo, *Storia del Santuario di Pompei* (Pompei, 1990), 59.

seated in glory at the right hand of the Father: this is the task of every follower of Christ and therefore the task of each one of us. In contemplating Christ's face we become open to receiving the mystery of Trinitarian life, experiencing ever anew the love of the Father and delighting in the joy of the Holy Spirit. Saint Paul's words can then be applied to us: "Beholding the glory of the Lord, we are being changed into his likeness, from one degree of glory to another; for this comes from the Lord who is the Spirit" (2 Cor 3:18).

Mary, Model of Contemplation

10. The contemplation of Christ has an *incomparable model* in Mary. In a unique way the face of the Son belongs to Mary. It was in her womb that Christ was formed, receiving from her a human resemblance which points to an even greater spiritual closeness. No one has ever devoted himself to the contemplation of the face of Christ as faithfully as Mary. The eyes of her heart already turned to him at the Annunciation, when she conceived him by the power of the Holy Spirit. In the months that followed she began to sense his presence and to picture his features. When at last she gave birth to him in Bethlehem, her eyes were able to gaze tenderly on the face of her Son, as she "wrapped him in swaddling cloths, and laid him in a manger" (Lk 2:7).

Thereafter Mary's gaze, ever filled with adoration and wonder, would never leave him. At times it would be *a questioning look*, as in the episode of the finding in the Temple: "Son, why have you treated us so?" (Lk 2:48); it would always be *a penetrating gaze*, one capable of deeply understanding Jesus, even to the point of perceiving his hidden feelings and anticipating his decisions, as at Cana (cf. Jn 2:5). At other times it would be *a look of sorrow*, especially beneath the Cross, where her vision would still be that of a mother giving birth, for Mary not only shared the passion and death of her Son, she also received the new son given to her in the beloved disciple (cf. Jn 19:26–27). On the morning of Easter hers would be *a gaze radiant with the joy of the Resurrection*, and finally, on the day of Pentecost, *a gaze afire* with the outpouring of the Spirit (cf. Acts 1:14).

Mary's Memories

11. Mary lived with her eyes fixed on Christ, treasuring his every word: "She kept all these things, pondering them in her heart" (Lk 2:19; cf. 2:51). The memories of Jesus, impressed upon her heart, were always with her, leading her to reflect on the various moments of her life at her Son's side. In a way those memories were to be the "rosary" which she recited uninterruptedly throughout her earthly life.

Even now, amid the joyful songs of the heavenly Jerusalem, the reasons for her thanksgiving and praise remain unchanged. They inspire her maternal concern for the pilgrim Church, in which she continues to relate her personal account of the Gospel. *Mary constantly sets before the faithful the "mysteries" of her Son*, with the desire that the contemplation of those mysteries will release all their saving power. In the recitation of the Rosary, the Christian community enters into contact with the memories and the contemplative gaze of Mary.

The Rosary, a Contemplative Prayer

12. The Rosary, precisely because it starts with Mary's own experience, is *an exquisitely contemplative prayer*. Without this contemplative dimension, it would lose its meaning, as Pope Paul VI clearly pointed out: "Without contemplation, the Rosary is a body without a soul, and its recitation runs the

risk of becoming a mechanical repetition of formulas, in violation of the admonition of Christ: 'In praying do not heap up empty phrases as the Gentiles do; for they think they will be heard for their many words' (Mt 6:7). By its nature the recitation of the Rosary calls for a quiet rhythm and a lingering pace, helping the individual to meditate on the mysteries of the Lord's life as seen through the eyes of her who was closest to the Lord. In this way the unfathomable riches of these mysteries are disclosed." [14]

It is worth pausing to consider this profound insight of Paul VI, in order to bring out certain aspects of the Rosary which show that it is really a form of Christocentric contemplation.

Remembering Christ with Mary

13. Mary's contemplation is above all *a remembering*. We need to understand this word in the biblical sense of remembrance (*zakar*) as a making present of the works brought about by God in the history of salvation. The Bible is an account of saving events culminating in Christ himself. These events not only belong to "yesterday"; *they are also part of the "today" of salvation*. This making present comes about above all in the Liturgy: what God accomplished centuries ago did not only affect the direct witnesses of those events; it continues to affect people in every age with its gift of grace. To some extent this is also true of every other devout approach to those events: to "remember" them in a spirit of faith and love is to be open to the grace which Christ won for us by the mysteries of his life, death and Resurrection.

Consequently, while it must be reaffirmed with the Second Vatican Council that the Liturgy, as the exercise of the

---

[14] Apostolic Exhortation *Marialis Cultus* (February 2, 1974), 47: AAS (1974), 156.

priestly office of Christ and an act of public worship, is "the summit to which the activity of the Church is directed and the font from which all its power flows",[15] it is also necessary to recall that the spiritual life "is not limited solely to participation in the Liturgy. Christians, while they are called to prayer in common, must also go to their own rooms to pray to their Father in secret (cf. Mt 6:6); indeed, according to the teaching of the Apostle, they must pray without ceasing (cf. 1 Thess 5:17)."[16] The Rosary, in its own particular way, is part of this varied panorama of "ceaseless" prayer. If the Liturgy, as the activity of Christ and the Church, is *a saving action par excellence*, the Rosary too, as a "meditation" with Mary on Christ, is *a salutary contemplation*. By immersing us in the mysteries of the Redeemer's life, it ensures that what he has done and what the Liturgy makes present is profoundly assimilated and shapes our existence.

Learning Christ from Mary

14. Christ is the supreme Teacher, the revealer and the one revealed. It is not just a question of learning what he taught but of *"learning him"*. In this regard could we have any better teacher than Mary? From the divine standpoint, the Spirit is the interior teacher who leads us to the full truth of Christ (cf. Jn 14:26; 15:26; 16:13). But among creatures no one knows Christ better than Mary; no one can introduce us to a profound knowledge of his mystery better than his Mother.

The first of the "signs" worked by Jesus—the changing of water into wine at the marriage in Cana—clearly presents Mary in the guise of a teacher, as she urges the servants to do what Jesus commands (cf. Jn 2:5). We can imagine that she would have done likewise for the disciples after Jesus' Ascen-

---

[15] Constitution on the Sacred Liturgy *Sacrosanctum Concilium*, 10.
[16] Ibid., 12.

sion, when she joined them in awaiting the Holy Spirit and supported them in their first mission. Contemplating the scenes of the Rosary in union with Mary is a means of learning from her to "read" Christ, to discover his secrets and to understand his message.

This school of Mary is all the more effective if we consider that she teaches by obtaining for us in abundance the gifts of the Holy Spirit, even as she offers us the incomparable example of her own "pilgrimage of faith".[17] As we contemplate each mystery of her Son's life, she invites us to do as she did at the Annunciation: to ask humbly the questions which open us to the light, in order to end with the obedience of faith: "Behold I am the handmaid of the Lord; be it done to me according to your word" (Lk 1:38).

Being Conformed to Christ with Mary

15. Christian spirituality is distinguished by the disciple's commitment to become conformed ever more fully to his Master (cf. Rom 8:29; Phil 3:10, 12). The outpouring of the Holy Spirit in Baptism grafts the believer like a branch onto the vine which is Christ (cf. Jn 15:5) and makes him a member of Christ's Mystical Body (cf. 1 Cor 12:12; Rom 12:5). This initial unity, however, calls for a growing assimilation which will increasingly shape the conduct of the disciple in accordance with the "mind" of Christ: "Have this mind among yourselves, which was in Christ Jesus" (Phil 2:5). In the words of the Apostle, we are called "to put on the Lord Jesus Christ" (cf. Rom 13:14; Gal 3:27).

In the spiritual journey of the Rosary, based on the constant contemplation—in Mary's company—of the face of Christ, this demanding ideal of being conformed to him is

[17] Second Vatican Ecumenical Council, Dogmatic Constitution on the Church *Lumen Gentium*, 58.

pursued through an association which could be described in terms of friendship. We are thereby enabled to enter naturally into Christ's life and as it were to share his deepest feelings. In this regard Blessed Bartolo Longo has written: "Just as two friends, frequently in each other's company, tend to develop similar habits, so too, by holding familiar converse with Jesus and the Blessed Virgin, by meditating on the mysteries of the Rosary and by living the same life in Holy Communion, we can become, to the extent of our lowliness, similar to them and can learn from these supreme models a life of humility, poverty, hiddenness, patience and perfection." [18]

In this process of being conformed to Christ in the Rosary, we entrust ourselves in a special way to the maternal care of the Blessed Virgin. She who is both the Mother of Christ and a member of the Church, indeed her "pre-eminent and altogether singular member",[19] is at the same time the "Mother of the Church". As such, she continually brings to birth children for the mystical Body of her Son. She does so through her intercession, imploring upon them the inexhaustible outpouring of the Spirit. Mary is *the perfect icon of the motherhood of the Church.*

The Rosary mystically transports us to Mary's side as she is busy watching over the human growth of Christ in the home of Nazareth. This enables her to train us and to mold us with the same care, until Christ is "fully formed" in us (cf. Gal 4:19). This role of Mary, totally grounded in that of Christ and radically subordinated to it, "in no way obscures or diminishes the unique mediation of Christ, but rather shows its power".[20] This is the luminous principle expressed by the Second Vatican Council which I have so powerfully experi-

[18] *I Quindici Sabati del Santissimo Rosario*, 27th ed. (Pompei, 1916), 27.

[19] Second Vatican Ecumenical Council, Dogmatic Constitution on the Church *Lumen Gentium*, 53.

[20] Ibid., 60.

enced in my own life and have made the basis of my episco-
pal motto: *Totus Tuus*.[21] The motto is of course inspired by the
teaching of Saint Louis Marie Grignion de Montfort, who
explained in the following words Mary's role in the process
of our configuration to Christ: "*Our entire perfection consists in
being conformed, united and consecrated to Jesus Christ. Hence the
most perfect of all devotions is undoubtedly that which conforms, unites and consecrates us most perfectly to Jesus
Christ. Now, since Mary is of all creatures the one most conformed to Jesus Christ, it follows that among all devotions
that which most consecrates and conforms a soul to our Lord
is devotion to Mary, his Holy Mother, and that the more a
soul is consecrated to her the more will it be consecrated to
Jesus Christ.*"[22] Never as in the Rosary do the life of Jesus and
that of Mary appear so deeply joined. Mary lives only in
Christ and for Christ!

Praying to Christ with Mary

16. Jesus invited us to turn to God with insistence and the
confidence that we will be heard: "Ask, and it will be given
to you; seek, and you will find; knock, and it will be opened
to you" (Mt 7:7). The basis for this power of prayer is the
goodness of the Father, but also the mediation of Christ
himself (cf. 1 Jn 2:1) and the working of the Holy Spirit who
"intercedes for us" according to the will of God (cf. Rom
8:26–27). For "we do not know how to pray as we ought"
(Rom 8:26), and at times we are not heard "because we ask
wrongly" (cf. Jas 4:2–3).

In support of the prayer which Christ and the Spirit cause
to rise in our hearts, Mary intervenes with her maternal

[21] Cf. First Radio Address *Urbi et Orbi* (October 17, 1978): AAS 70 (1978), 927.

[22] *Treatise on True Devotion to the Blessed Virgin Mary.*

intercession. "The prayer of the Church is sustained by the prayer of Mary." [23] If Jesus, the one Mediator, is the Way of our prayer, then Mary, his purest and most transparent reflection, shows us the Way. "Beginning with Mary's unique cooperation with the working of the Holy Spirit, the Churches developed their prayer to the Holy Mother of God, centering it on the person of Christ manifested in his mysteries." [24] At the wedding of Cana the Gospel clearly shows the power of Mary's intercession as she makes known to Jesus the needs of others: "They have no wine" (Jn 2:3).

The Rosary is both meditation and supplication. Insistent prayer to the Mother of God is based on confidence that her maternal intercession can obtain all things from the heart of her Son. She is "all-powerful by grace", to use the bold expression, which needs to be properly understood, of Blessed Bartolo Longo in his *Supplication to Our Lady*.[25] This is a conviction which, beginning with the Gospel, has grown ever more firm in the experience of the Christian people. The supreme poet Dante expresses it marvelously in the lines sung by Saint Bernard: "Lady, thou art so great and so powerful, that whoever desires grace yet does not turn to thee, would have his desire fly without wings." [26] When in the Rosary we plead with Mary, the sanctuary of the Holy Spirit (cf. Lk 1:35), she intercedes for us before the Father who filled her with grace and before the Son born of her womb, praying with us and for us.

[23] *Catechism of the Catholic Church*, 2679.

[24] Ibid., 2675.

[25] The *Supplication to the Queen of the Holy Rosary* was composed by Blessed Bartolo Longo in 1883 in response to the appeal of Pope Leo XIII, made in his first Encyclical on the Rosary, for the spiritual commitment of all Catholics in combating social ills. It is solemnly recited twice yearly, in May and October.

[26] *Divina Commedia*, Paradiso XXXIII, 13–15.

Proclaiming Christ with Mary

17. The Rosary is also *a path of proclamation and increasing knowledge*, in which the mystery of Christ is presented again and again at different levels of the Christian experience. Its form is that of a prayerful and contemplative presentation, capable of forming Christians according to the heart of Christ. When the recitation of the Rosary combines all the elements needed for an effective meditation, especially in its communal celebration in parishes and shrines, it can present *a significant catechetical opportunity* which pastors should use to advantage. In this way too Our Lady of the Rosary continues her work of proclaiming Christ. The history of the Rosary shows how this prayer was used in particular by the Dominicans at a difficult time for the Church due to the spread of heresy. Today we are facing new challenges. Why should we not once more have recourse to the Rosary, with the same faith as those who have gone before us? The Rosary retains all its power and continues to be a valuable pastoral resource for every good evangelizer.

CHAPTER II

MYSTERIES OF CHRIST— MYSTERIES OF HIS MOTHER

The Rosary, "a Compendium of the Gospel"

18. The only way to approach the contemplation of Christ's face is by listening in the Spirit to the Father's voice, since "no one knows the Son except the Father" (Mt 11:27). In the region of Caesarea Philippi, Jesus responded to Peter's confession of faith by indicating the source of that clear

intuition of his identity: "Flesh and blood has not revealed this to you, but my Father who is in heaven" (Mt 16:17). What is needed, then, is a revelation from above. In order to receive that revelation, attentive listening is indispensable: "Only *the experience of silence and prayer* offers the proper setting for the growth and development of a true, faithful and consistent knowledge of that mystery." [27]

The Rosary is one of the traditional paths of Christian prayer directed to the contemplation of Christ's face. Pope Paul VI described it in these words: "As a Gospel prayer, centered on the mystery of the redemptive Incarnation, the Rosary is a prayer with a clearly Christological orientation. Its most characteristic element, in fact, the litany-like succession of Hail Marys, becomes in itself an unceasing praise of Christ, who is the ultimate object both of the Angel's announcement and of the greeting of the Mother of John the Baptist: 'Blessed is the fruit of your womb' (Lk 1:42). We would go further and say that the succession of Hail Marys constitutes the warp on which is woven the contemplation of the mysteries. The Jesus that each Hail Mary recalls is the same Jesus whom the succession of mysteries proposes to us now as the Son of God, now as the Son of the Virgin." [28]

A Proposed Addition to the Traditional Pattern

19. Of the many mysteries of Christ's life, only a few are indicated by the Rosary in the form that has become generally established with the seal of the Church's approval. The selection was determined by the origin of the prayer, which

[27] John Paul II, Apostolic Letter *Novo Millennio Ineunte* (January 6, 2001), 20: AAS 93 (2001), 279.

[28] Apostolic Exhortation *Marialis Cultus* (February 2, 1974), 46: AAS 6 (1974), 155.

was based on the number 150, the number of the psalms in the Psalter.

I believe, however, that to bring out fully the Christological depth of the Rosary it would be suitable to make an addition to the traditional pattern which, while left to the freedom of individuals and communities, could broaden it to include *the mysteries of Christ's public ministry between his Baptism and his Passion*. In the course of those mysteries we contemplate important aspects of the person of Christ as the definitive revelation of God. Declared the beloved Son of the Father at the Baptism in the Jordan, Christ is the one who announces the coming of the Kingdom, bears witness to it in his works and proclaims its demands. It is during the years of his public ministry that *the mystery of Christ is most evidently a mystery of light*: "While I am in the world, I am the light of the world" (Jn 9:5).

Consequently, for the Rosary to become more fully a "compendium of the Gospel", it is fitting to add, following reflection on the Incarnation and the hidden life of Christ (*the joyful mysteries*) and before focusing on the sufferings of his Passion (*the sorrowful mysteries*) and the triumph of his Resurrection (*the glorious mysteries*), a meditation on certain particularly significant moments in his public ministry (*the mysteries of light*). This addition of these new mysteries, without prejudice to any essential aspect of the prayer's traditional format, is meant to give it fresh life and to enkindle renewed interest in the Rosary's place within Christian spirituality as a true doorway to the depths of the Heart of Christ, ocean of joy and of light, of suffering and of glory.

The Joyful Mysteries

20. The first five decades, the "joyful mysteries", are marked by *the joy radiating from the event of the Incarnation*. This is

clear from the very first mystery, the Annunciation, where Gabriel's greeting to the Virgin of Nazareth is linked to an invitation to messianic joy: "Rejoice, Mary". The whole of salvation history, in some sense the entire history of the world, has led up to this greeting. If it is the Father's plan to unite all things in Christ (cf. Eph 1:10), then the whole of the universe is in some way touched by the divine favor with which the Father looks upon Mary and makes her the Mother of his Son. The whole of humanity, in turn, is embraced by the *fiat* with which she readily agrees to the will of God.

Exultation is the keynote of the encounter with Elizabeth, where the sound of Mary's voice and the presence of Christ in her womb cause John to "leap for joy" (cf. Lk 1:44). Gladness also fills the scene in Bethlehem, when the birth of the divine Child, the Savior of the world, is announced by the song of the angels and proclaimed to the shepherds as "news of great joy" (Lk 2:10).

The final two mysteries, while preserving this climate of joy, already point to the drama yet to come. The Presentation in the Temple not only expresses the joy of the Child's consecration and the ecstasy of the aged Simeon; it also records the prophecy that Christ will be a "sign of contradiction" for Israel and that a sword will pierce his mother's heart (cf. Lk 2:34–35). Joy mixed with drama marks the fifth mystery, the finding of the twelve-year-old Jesus in the Temple. Here he appears in his divine wisdom as he listens and raises questions, already in effect one who "teaches". The revelation of his mystery as the Son wholly dedicated to his Father's affairs proclaims the radical nature of the Gospel, in which even the closest of human relationships are challenged by the absolute demands of the Kingdom. Mary and Joseph, fearful and anxious, "did not understand" his words (Lk 2:50).

To meditate upon the "joyful" mysteries, then, is to enter

into the ultimate causes and the deepest meaning of Christian joy. It is to focus on the realism of the mystery of the Incarnation and on the obscure foreshadowing of the mystery of the saving Passion. Mary leads us to discover the secret of Christian joy, reminding us that Christianity is, first and foremost, *euangelion*, "good news", which has as its heart and its whole content the person of Jesus Christ, the Word made flesh, the one Savior of the world.

The Mysteries of Light

21. Moving on from the infancy and the hidden life in Nazareth to the public life of Jesus, our contemplation brings us to those mysteries which may be called in a special way "mysteries of light". Certainly the whole mystery of Christ is a mystery of light. He is the "light of the world" (Jn 8:12). Yet this truth emerges in a special way during the years of his public life, when he proclaims the Gospel of the Kingdom. In proposing to the Christian community five significant moments—"luminous" mysteries—during this phase of Christ's life, I think that the following can be fittingly singled out: (1) his Baptism in the Jordan, (2) his self-manifestation at the wedding of Cana, (3) his proclamation of the Kingdom of God, with his call to conversion, (4) his Transfiguration, and finally, (5) his institution of the Eucharist, as the sacramental expression of the Paschal Mystery.

Each of these mysteries is *a revelation of the Kingdom now present in the very person of Jesus*. The Baptism in the Jordan is first of all a mystery of light. Here, as Christ descends into the waters, the innocent one who became "sin" for our sake (cf. 2 Cor 5:21), the heavens open wide and the voice of the Father declares him the beloved Son (cf. Mt 3:17 and parallels), while the Spirit descends on him to invest him with the mission which he is to carry out. Another mystery of light is the first of the signs, given at Cana (cf. Jn 2:1–12), when Christ changes water into wine and opens the hearts of the disciples to faith, thanks to the intervention of Mary, the first among believers. Another mystery of light is the preaching by which Jesus proclaims the coming of the Kingdom of God, calls to conversion (cf. Mk 1:15) and forgives the sins of all who draw near to him in humble trust (cf. Mk 2:3–13; Lk 7:47–48): the inauguration of that ministry of mercy which he continues to exercise until the end of the world, particularly through the Sacrament of Reconciliation which he has entrusted to his Church (cf. Jn 20:22–23). The mystery of light *par excellence* is the Transfiguration, traditionally believed to have taken place on Mount Tabor. The glory of the Godhead shines forth from the face of Christ as the Father commands the astonished Apostles to "listen to him" (cf. Lk 9:35 and parallels) and to prepare to experience with him the agony of the Passion, so as to come with him to the joy of the Resurrection and a life transfigured by the Holy Spirit. A final mystery of light is the institution of the Eucharist, in which Christ offers his body and blood as food under the signs of bread and wine, and testifies "to the end" his love for humanity (Jn 13:1), for whose salvation he will offer himself in sacrifice.

In these mysteries, apart from the miracle at Cana, *the presence of Mary remains in the background*. The Gospels make only the briefest reference to her occasional presence at one moment or other during the preaching of Jesus (cf. Mk 3:31–5; Jn 2:12), and they give no indication that she was present at the Last Supper and the institution of the Eucharist. Yet the role she assumed at Cana in some way accompanies Christ throughout his ministry. The revelation made directly by the Father at the Baptism in the Jordan and echoed by John the Baptist is placed upon Mary's lips at Cana, and it becomes the great maternal counsel which Mary addresses to the Church of every age: "Do whatever he tells you" (Jn 2:5). This counsel is a fitting introduction to the words and signs of Christ's public ministry and it forms the Marian foundation of all the "mysteries of light".

The Sorrowful Mysteries

22. The Gospels give great prominence to the sorrowful mysteries of Christ. From the beginning Christian piety, especially during the Lenten devotion of the *Way of the Cross*, has focused on the individual moments of the Passion, realizing that here is found *the culmination of the revelation of God's love* and the source of our salvation. The Rosary selects certain moments from the Passion, inviting the faithful to contemplate them in their hearts and to relive them. The sequence of meditations begins with Gethsemane, where Christ experiences a moment of great anguish before the will of the Father, against which the weakness of the flesh would be tempted to rebel. There Jesus encounters all the temptations and confronts all the sins of humanity, in order to say to the Father: "Not my will but yours be done" (Lk 22:42 and parallels). This "Yes" of Christ reverses the "No" of our first parents in the Garden of Eden. And the cost of this faithfulness to the Father's will is made clear in the following mysteries; by his scourging, his crowning with thorns, his carrying the Cross and his death on the Cross, the Lord is cast into the most abject suffering: *Ecce homo!*

This abject suffering reveals not only the love of God but also the meaning of man himself.

Ecce homo: the meaning, origin and fulfillment of man is to be found in Christ, the God who humbles himself out of love "even unto death, death on a cross" (Phil 2:8). The sorrowful mysteries help the believer to relive the death of Jesus, to stand at the foot of the Cross beside Mary, to enter with her into the depths of God's love for man and to experience all its life-giving power.

The Glorious Mysteries

23. "The contemplation of Christ's face cannot stop at the image of the Crucified One. He is the Risen One!" [29] The Rosary has always expressed this knowledge born of faith and invited the believer to pass beyond the darkness of the Passion in order to gaze upon Christ's glory in the Resurrection and Ascension. Contemplating the Risen One, Christians *rediscover the reasons for their own faith* (cf. 1 Cor 15:14) and relive the joy not only of those to whom Christ appeared—the Apostles, Mary Magdalene and the disciples on the road to Emmaus—but also *the joy of Mary*, who must have had an equally intense experience of the new life of her glorified Son. In the Ascension, Christ was raised in glory to the right hand of the Father, while Mary herself would be raised to that same glory in the Assumption, enjoying beforehand, by a unique privilege, the destiny reserved for all the just at the resurrection of the dead. Crowned in glory – as she appears in the last glorious mystery – Mary shines forth as Queen of the Angels and Saints, the anticipation and the supreme realization of the eschatological state of the Church.

At the center of this unfolding sequence of the glory of the Son and the Mother, the Rosary sets before us the third glorious mystery, Pentecost, which reveals the face of the Church as a family gathered together with Mary, enlivened by the powerful outpouring of the Spirit and ready for the mission of evangelization. The contemplation of this scene, like that of the other glorious mysteries, ought to lead the faithful to an ever greater appreciation of their new life in

[29] John Paul II, Apostolic Letter *Novo Millennio Ineunte* (January 6, 2001), 28: AAS 93 (2001), 284.

Christ, lived in the heart of the Church, a life of which the scene of Pentecost itself is the great "icon". The glorious mysteries thus lead the faithful to *greater hope for the eschatological goal* towards which they journey as members of the pilgrim People of God in history. This can only impel them to bear courageous witness to that "good news" which gives meaning to their entire existence.

From "Mysteries" to the "Mystery": Mary's Way

24. The cycles of meditation proposed by the Holy Rosary are by no means exhaustive, but they do bring to mind what is essential and they awaken in the soul a thirst for a knowledge of Christ continually nourished by the pure source of the Gospel. Every individual event in the life of Christ, as narrated by the Evangelists, is resplendent with the Mystery that surpasses all understanding (cf. Eph 3:19): the Mystery of the Word made flesh, in whom "all the fullness of God dwells bodily" (Col 2:9). For this reason the *Catechism of the Catholic Church* places great emphasis on the mysteries of Christ, pointing out that "everything in the life of Jesus is a sign of his Mystery."[30] The *"duc in altum"* of the Church of the third millennium will be determined by the ability of Christians to enter into the "perfect knowledge of God's mystery, of Christ, in whom are hidden all the treasures of wisdom and knowledge" (Col 2:2–3). The Letter to the Ephesians makes this heartfelt prayer for all the baptized: "May Christ dwell in your hearts through faith, so that you, being rooted and grounded in love, may have power... to know the love of Christ which surpasses knowledge, that you may be filled with all the fullness of God" (3:17–19).

[30] No. 515.

The Rosary is at the service of this ideal; it offers the "secret" which leads easily to a profound and inward knowledge of Christ. We might call it *Mary's way*. It is the way of the example of the Virgin of Nazareth, a woman of faith, of silence, of attentive listening. It is also the way of a Marian devotion inspired by knowledge of the inseparable bond between Christ and his Blessed Mother: *the mysteries of Christ* are also in some sense *the mysteries of his Mother*, even when they do not involve her directly, for she lives from him and through him. By making our own the words of the Angel Gabriel and Saint Elizabeth contained in the Hail Mary, we find ourselves constantly drawn to seek out afresh in Mary, in her arms and in her heart, the "blessed fruit of her womb" (cf. Lk 1:42).

Mystery of Christ, Mystery of Man

25. In my testimony of 1978 mentioned above, where I described the Rosary as my favorite prayer, I used an idea to which I would like to return. I said then that "the simple prayer of the Rosary marks the rhythm of human life." [31]

In the light of what has been said so far on the mysteries of Christ, it is not difficult to go deeper into this *anthropological significance* of the Rosary, which is far deeper than may appear at first sight. Anyone who contemplates Christ through the various stages of his life cannot fail to perceive in him *the truth about man*. This is the great affirmation of the Second Vatican Council which I have so often discussed in my own teaching since the Encyclical Letter *Redemptor Hominis*: "It is only in the mystery of the Word made flesh that the mystery of man is seen in its true light." [32] The

[31] Angelus Message of October 29, 1978: *Insegnamenti*, I (1978), 76.
[32] Second Vatican Ecumenical Council, Pastoral Constitution on the Church in the Modern World *Gaudium et Spes*, 22.

Rosary helps to open up the way to this light. Following in the path of Christ, in whom man's path is "recapitulated",[33] revealed and redeemed, believers come face to face with the image of the true man. Contemplating Christ's birth, they learn of the sanctity of life; seeing the household of Nazareth, they learn the original truth of the family according to God's plan; listening to the Master in the mysteries of his public ministry, they find the light which leads them to enter the Kingdom of God; and following him on the way to Calvary, they learn the meaning of salvific suffering. Finally, contemplating Christ and his Blessed Mother in glory, they see the goal towards which each of us is called, if we allow ourselves to be healed and transformed by the Holy Spirit. It could be said that each mystery of the Rosary, carefully meditated, sheds light on the mystery of man.

At the same time, it becomes natural to bring to this encounter with the sacred humanity of the Redeemer all the problems, anxieties, labors and endeavors which go to make up our lives. "Cast your burden on the Lord and he will sustain you" (Ps 55:23). To pray the Rosary is to hand over our burdens to the merciful hearts of Christ and his Mother. Twenty-five years later, thinking back over the difficulties which have also been part of my exercise of the Petrine ministry, I feel the need to say once more, as a warm invitation to everyone to experience it personally: the Rosary does indeed "mark the rhythm of human life", bringing it into harmony with the "rhythm" of God's own life, in the joyful communion of the Holy Trinity, our life's destiny and deepest longing.

---

[33] Cf. Saint Irenaeus of Lyons, *Adversus Haereses*, III, 18, 1: PG 7, 932.

CHAPTER III

"FOR ME TO LIVE IS CHRIST"

The Rosary, a Way of Assimilating the Mystery

26. Meditation on the mysteries of Christ is proposed in the Rosary by means of a method designed to assist in their assimilation. It is a method *based on repetition*. This applies above all to the Hail Mary, repeated ten times in each mystery. If this repetition is considered superficially, there could be a temptation to see the Rosary as a dry and boring exercise. It is quite another thing, however, when the Rosary is thought of as an outpouring of that love which tirelessly returns to the person loved with expressions similar in their content but ever fresh in terms of the feeling pervading them.

In Christ, God has truly assumed a "heart of flesh". Not only does God have a divine heart, rich in mercy and in forgiveness, but also a human heart, capable of all the stirrings of affection. If we needed evidence for this from the Gospel, we could easily find it in the touching dialogue between Christ and Peter after the Resurrection: "Simon, son of John, do you love me?" Three times this question is put to Peter, and three times he gives the reply: "Lord, you know that I love you" (cf. Jn 21:15–17). Over and above the specific meaning of this passage, so important for Peter's mission, none can fail to recognize the beauty of this triple repetition, in which the insistent request and the corresponding reply are expressed in terms familiar from the universal experience of human love. To understand the Rosary, one has to enter into the psychological dynamic proper to love.

One thing is clear: although the repeated Hail Mary is addressed directly to Mary, it is to Jesus that the act of love is ultimately directed, with her and through her. The repetition is nourished by the desire to be conformed ever more completely to Christ, the true program of the Christian life. Saint Paul expressed this project with words of fire: "For me to live is Christ and to die is gain" (Phil 1:21). And again: "It is no longer I that live, but Christ lives in me" (Gal 2:20). The Rosary helps us to be conformed ever more closely to Christ until we attain true holiness.

A Valid Method . . .

27. We should not be surprised that our relationship with Christ makes use of a method. God communicates himself to us respecting our human nature and its vital rhythms. Hence, while Christian spirituality is familiar with the most sublime forms of mystical silence in which images, words and gestures are all, so to speak, superseded by an intense and ineffable union with God, it normally engages the whole person in all his complex psychological, physical and relational reality.

This becomes apparent *in the Liturgy*. Sacraments and sacramentals are structured as a series of rites which bring into play all the dimensions of the person. The same applies to non-liturgical prayer. This is confirmed by the fact that, in the East, the most characteristic prayer of Christological meditation, centered on the words "Lord Jesus Christ, Son of God, have mercy on me, a sinner",[34] is traditionally linked to the rhythm of breathing; while this practice favors perseverance in the prayer, it also in some way embodies the desire for Christ to become the breath, the soul and the "all" of one's life.

. . . Which Can Nevertheless Be Improved

28. I mentioned in my Apostolic Letter *Novo Millennio Ineunte* that the West is now experiencing *a renewed demand*

---

[34] *Catechism of the Catholic Church,* 2616.

for meditation, which at times leads to a keen interest in aspects of other religions.[35] Some Christians, limited in their knowledge of the Christian contemplative tradition, are attracted by those forms of prayer. While the latter contain many elements which are positive and at times compatible with Christian experience, they are often based on ultimately unacceptable premises. Much in vogue among these approaches are methods aimed at attaining a high level of spiritual concentration by using techniques of a psychophysical, repetitive and symbolic nature. The Rosary is situated within this broad gamut of religious phenomena, but it is distinguished by characteristics of its own which correspond to specifically Christian requirements.

In effect, the Rosary is simply *a method of contemplation*. As a method, it serves as a means to an end and cannot become an end in itself. All the same, as the fruit of centuries of experience, this method should not be undervalued. In its favor one could cite the experience of countless Saints. This is not to say, however, that the method cannot be improved. Such is the intent of the addition of the new series of *mysteria lucis* to the overall cycle of mysteries and of the few suggestions which I am proposing in this Letter regarding its manner of recitation. These suggestions, while respecting the well-established structure of this prayer, are intended to help the faithful to understand it in the richness of its symbolism and in harmony with the demands of daily life. Otherwise there is a risk that the Rosary would not only fail to produce the intended spiritual effects, but even that the beads, with which it is usually said, could come to be regarded as some kind of amulet or magic object, thereby radically distorting their meaning and function.

[35] Cf. no. 33: AAS 93 (2001), 289.

Announcing Each Mystery

29. Announcing each mystery, and perhaps even using a suitable icon to portray it, is as it were *to open up a scenario* on which to focus our attention. The words direct the imagination and the mind towards a particular episode or moment in the life of Christ. In the Church's traditional spirituality, the veneration of icons and the many devotions appealing to the senses, as well as the method of prayer proposed by Saint Ignatius of Loyola in the Spiritual Exercises, make use of visual and imaginative elements (the *compositio loci*), judged to be of great help in concentrating the mind on the particular mystery. This is a methodology, moreover, which *corresponds to the inner logic of the Incarnation*: in Jesus, God wanted to take on human features. It is through his bodily reality that we are led into contact with the mystery of his divinity.

This need for concreteness finds further expression in the announcement of the various mysteries of the Rosary. Obviously these mysteries neither replace the Gospel nor exhaust its content. The Rosary, therefore, is no substitute for *lectio divina*; on the contrary, it presupposes and promotes it. Yet, even though the mysteries contemplated in the Rosary, even with the addition of the *mysteria lucis*, do no more than outline the fundamental elements of the life of Christ, they easily draw the mind to a more expansive reflection on the rest of the Gospel, especially when the Rosary is prayed in a setting of prolonged recollection.

Listening to the Word of God

30. In order to supply a biblical foundation and greater depth to our meditation, it is helpful to follow the announcement of the mystery with *the proclamation of a related biblical passage*, long or short, depending on the circumstances. No

other words can ever match the efficacy of the inspired word. As we listen, we are certain that this is the word of God, spoken for today and spoken "for me".

If received in this way, the word of God can become part of the Rosary's methodology of repetition without giving rise to the ennui derived from the simple recollection of something already well known. It is not a matter of recalling information but *of allowing God to speak.* In certain solemn communal celebrations, this word can be appropriately illustrated by a brief commentary.

Silence

31. *Listening and meditation are nourished by silence.* After the announcement of the mystery and the proclamation of the word, it is fitting to pause and focus one's attention for a suitable period of time on the mystery concerned, before moving into vocal prayer. A discovery of the importance of silence is one of the secrets of practicing contemplation and meditation. One drawback of a society dominated by technology and the mass media is the fact that silence becomes increasingly difficult to achieve. Just as moments of silence are recommended in the Liturgy, so too in the recitation of the Rosary it is fitting to pause briefly after listening to the word of God, while the mind focuses on the content of a particular mystery.

The "Our Father"

32. After listening to the word and focusing on the mystery, it is natural for *the mind to be lifted up towards the Father.* In each of his mysteries, Jesus always leads us to the Father, for as he rests in the Father's bosom (cf. Jn 1:18) he is continually turned towards him. He wants us to share in his intimacy

with the Father, so that we can say with him: "Abba, Father" (Rom 8:15; Gal 4:6). By virtue of his relationship to the Father he makes us brothers and sisters of himself and of one another, communicating to us the Spirit which is both his and the Father's. Acting as a kind of foundation for the Christological and Marian meditation which unfolds in the repetition of the Hail Mary, the Our Father makes meditation upon the mystery, even when carried out in solitude, an ecclesial experience.

The Ten "Hail Marys"

33. This is the most substantial element in the Rosary and also the one which makes it a Marian prayer *par excellence*. Yet when the Hail Mary is properly understood, we come to see clearly that its Marian character is not opposed to its Christological character, but that it actually emphasizes and increases it. The first part of the Hail Mary, drawn from the words spoken to Mary by the Angel Gabriel and by Saint Elizabeth, is a contemplation in adoration of the mystery accomplished in the Virgin of Nazareth. These words express, so to speak, the wonder of heaven and earth; they could be said to give us a glimpse of God's own wonderment as he contemplates his "masterpiece"—the Incarnation of the Son in the womb of the Virgin Mary. If we recall how, in the Book of Genesis, God "saw all that he had made" (Gen 1:31), we can find here an echo of that "pathos with which God, at the dawn of creation, looked upon the work of his hands".[36] The repetition of the Hail Mary in the Rosary gives us a share in God's own wonder and pleasure: in jubilant amazement we acknowledge the greatest miracle of history. Mary's prophecy here finds its

---

[36] John Paul II, *Letter to Artists* (April 4, 1999), 1: AAS 91 (1999), 1155.

fulfillment: "Henceforth all generations will call me blessed" (Lk 1:48).

The center of gravity in the Hail Mary, the hinge as it were which joins its two parts, is *the name of Jesus*. Sometimes, in hurried recitation, this center of gravity can be overlooked, and with it the connection to the mystery of Christ being contemplated. Yet it is precisely the emphasis given to the name of Jesus and to his mystery that is the sign of a meaningful and fruitful recitation of the Rosary. Pope Paul VI drew attention, in his Apostolic Exhortation *Marialis Cultus*, to the custom in certain regions of highlighting the name of Christ by the addition of a clause referring to the mystery being contemplated.[37] This is a praiseworthy custom, especially during public recitation. It gives forceful expression to our faith in Christ, directed to the different moments of the Redeemer's life. It is at once *a profession of faith* and an aid in concentrating our meditation, since it facilitates the process of assimilation to the mystery of Christ inherent in the repetition of the Hail Mary. When we repeat the name of Jesus—the only name given to us by which we may hope for salvation (cf. Acts 4:12)—in close association with the name of his Blessed Mother, almost as if it were done at her suggestion, we set out on a path of assimilation meant to help us enter more deeply into the life of Christ.

From Mary's uniquely privileged relationship with Christ, which makes her the Mother of God, *Theotókos*, derives the forcefulness of the appeal we make to her in the second half of the prayer, as we entrust to her maternal intercession our lives and the hour of our death.

---

[37] Cf. no. 46: AAS 66 (1974), 155. This custom has also been recently praised by the Congregation for Divine Worship and for the Discipline of the Sacraments in its *Direttorio su pietà popolare e liturgia. Principi e orientamenti* (December 17, 2001), 201, Vatican City, 2002, 165.

The "Gloria"

34. Trinitarian doxology is the goal of all Christian contemplation. For Christ is the way that leads us to the Father in the Spirit. If we travel this way to the end, we repeatedly encounter the mystery of the three divine Persons, to whom all praise, worship and thanksgiving are due. It is important that the *Gloria, the high-point of contemplation*, be given due prominence in the Rosary. In public recitation it could be sung, as a way of giving proper emphasis to the essentially Trinitarian structure of all Christian prayer.

To the extent that meditation on the mystery is attentive and profound, and to the extent that it is enlivened—from one Hail Mary to another—by love for Christ and for Mary, the glorification of the Trinity at the end of each decade, far from being a perfunctory conclusion, takes on its proper contemplative tone, raising the mind as it were to the heights of heaven and enabling us in some way to relive the experience of Tabor, a foretaste of the contemplation yet to come: "It is good for us to be here!" (Lk 9:33).

The Concluding Short Prayer

35. In current practice, the Trinitarian doxology is followed by a brief concluding prayer which varies according to local custom. Without in any way diminishing the value of such invocations, it is worthwhile to note that the contemplation of the mysteries could better express their full spiritual fruitfulness if an effort were made to conclude each mystery with *a prayer for the fruits specific to that particular mystery*. In this way the Rosary would better express its connection with the Christian life. One fine liturgical prayer suggests as much, inviting us to pray that, by meditation on the mysteries of the

Rosary, we may come to "imitate what they contain and obtain what they promise".[38]

Such a final prayer could take on a legitimate variety of forms, as indeed it already does. In this way the Rosary can be better adapted to different spiritual traditions and different Christian communities. It is to be hoped, then, that appropriate formulas will be widely circulated, after due pastoral discernment and possibly after experimental use in centers and shrines particularly devoted to the Rosary, so that the People of God may benefit from an abundance of authentic spiritual riches and find nourishment for their personal contemplation.

The Rosary Beads

36. The traditional aid used for the recitation of the Rosary is the set of beads. At the most superficial level, the beads often become a simple counting mechanism to mark the succession of Hail Marys. Yet they can also take on a symbolism which can give added depth to contemplation.

Here the first thing to note is the way *the beads converge upon the Crucifix*, which both opens and closes the unfolding sequence of prayer. The life and prayer of believers is centered upon Christ. Everything begins from him, everything leads towards him, everything, through him, in the Holy Spirit, attains to the Father.

As a counting mechanism, marking the progress of the prayer, the beads evoke the unending path of contemplation and of Christian perfection. Blessed Bartolo Longo saw them also as a "chain" which links us to God. A chain, yes, but a sweet chain; for sweet indeed is the bond to God who is also

---

[38] ". . . concede, quaesumus, ut haec mysteria sacratissimo beatae Mariae Virginis Rosario recolentes, et imitemur quod continent, et quod promittunt assequamur." Missale Romanum 1960, in festo B.M. Virginis a Rosario.

our Father. A "filial" chain which puts us in tune with Mary, the "handmaid of the Lord" (Lk 1:38), and, most of all, with Christ himself, who, though he was in the form of God, made himself a "servant" out of love for us (Phil 2:7).

A fine way to expand the symbolism of the beads is to let them remind us of our many relationships, of the bond of communion and fraternity which unites us all in Christ.

The Opening and Closing

37. At present, in different parts of the Church, there are many ways to introduce the Rosary. In some places, it is customary to begin with the opening words of Psalm 70: "O God, come to my aid; O Lord, make haste to help me", as if to nourish in those who are praying a humble awareness of their own insufficiency. In other places, the Rosary begins with the recitation of the Creed, as if to make the profession of faith the basis of the contemplative journey about to be undertaken. These and similar customs, to the extent that they prepare the mind for contemplation, are all equally legitimate. The Rosary is then ended with a prayer for the intentions of the Pope, as if to expand the vision of the one praying to embrace all the needs of the Church. It is precisely in order to encourage this ecclesial dimension of the Rosary that the Church has seen fit to grant indulgences to those who recite it with the required dispositions.

If prayed in this way, the Rosary truly becomes a spiritual itinerary in which Mary acts as Mother, Teacher and Guide, sustaining the faithful by her powerful intercession. Is it any wonder, then, that the soul feels the need, after saying this prayer and experiencing so profoundly the motherhood of Mary, to burst forth in praise of the Blessed Virgin, either in that splendid prayer the *Salve Regina* or in the *Litany of Loreto*? This is the crowning moment of an inner journey which has brought the faithful into living contact with the mystery of Christ and his Blessed Mother.

Distribution over Time

38. The Rosary can be recited in full every day, and there are those who most laudably do so. In this way it fills with prayer the days of many a contemplative, or keeps company with the sick and the elderly who have abundant time at their disposal. Yet it is clear—and this applies all the more if the new series of *mysteria lucis* is included—that many people will not be able to recite more than a part of the Rosary, according to a certain weekly pattern. This weekly distribution has the effect of giving the different days of the week a certain spiritual "color", by analogy with the way in which the Liturgy colors the different seasons of the liturgical year.

According to current practice, Monday and Thursday are dedicated to the "joyful mysteries", Tuesday and Friday to the "sorrowful mysteries", and Wednesday, Saturday and Sunday to the "glorious mysteries". Where might the "mysteries of light" be inserted? If we consider that the "glorious mysteries" are said on both Saturday and Sunday, and that Saturday has always had a special Marian flavor, the second weekly meditation on the "joyful mysteries", mysteries in which Mary's presence is especially pronounced, could be moved to Saturday. Thursday would then be free for meditating on the "mysteries of light".

This indication is not intended to limit a rightful freedom in personal and community prayer, where account needs to be taken of spiritual and pastoral needs and of the occurrence of particular liturgical celebrations which might call for suitable adaptations. What is really important is that the Rosary should always be seen and experienced as a path of contemplation. In the Rosary, in a way similar to what takes place in the Liturgy, the Christian week, centered on Sunday, the day of Resurrection, becomes a journey through the mysteries of the life of Christ, and he is revealed in the lives of his disciples as the Lord of time and of history.

CONCLUSION

"Blessed Rosary of Mary, Sweet Chain Linking Us to God"

39. What has been said so far makes abundantly clear the richness of this traditional prayer, which has the simplicity of a popular devotion but also the theological depth of a prayer suited to those who feel the need for deeper contemplation.

The Church has always attributed particular efficacy to this prayer, entrusting to the Rosary, to its choral recitation and to its constant practice, the most difficult problems. At times when Christianity itself seemed under threat, its deliverance was attributed to the power of this prayer, and Our Lady of the Rosary was acclaimed as the one whose intercession brought salvation.

Today I willingly entrust to the power of this prayer—as I mentioned at the beginning—the cause of peace in the world and the cause of the family.

Peace

40. The grave challenges confronting the world at the start of this new Millennium lead us to think that only an intervention from on high, capable of guiding the hearts of those living in situations of conflict and those governing the destinies of nations, can give reason to hope for a brighter future.

The Rosary is by its nature a prayer for peace, since it consists in the contemplation of Christ, the Prince of Peace, the one who is "our peace" (Eph 2:14). Anyone who assimilates the mystery of Christ—and this is clearly the goal of the Rosary—learns the secret of peace and makes it his life's project. Moreover, by virtue of its meditative character, with the tranquil succession of Hail Marys, the Rosary has a peaceful effect on those who pray it, disposing them to receive and experience in their innermost depths, and to spread around them, that true peace which is the special gift of the Risen Lord (cf. Jn 14:27; 20–21).

The Rosary is also a prayer for peace because of the fruits of charity which it produces. When prayed well in a truly meditative way, the Rosary leads to an encounter with Christ in his mysteries and so cannot fail to draw attention to the face of Christ in others, especially in the most afflicted. How could one possibly contemplate the mystery of the Child of Bethlehem, in the joyful mysteries, without experiencing the desire to welcome, defend and promote life, and to shoulder the burdens of suffering children all over the world? How could one possibly follow in the footsteps of Christ the Revealer, in the mysteries of light, without resolving to bear witness to his "Beatitudes" in daily life? And how could one contemplate Christ carrying the Cross and Christ Crucified, without feeling the need to act as a "Simon of Cyrene" for our brothers and sisters weighed down by grief or crushed by despair? Finally, how could one possibly gaze upon the glory of the Risen Christ or of Mary Queen of Heaven, without yearning to make this world more beautiful, more just, more closely conformed to God's plan?

In a word, by focusing our eyes on Christ, the Rosary also makes us peacemakers in the world. By its nature as an insistent choral petition in harmony with Christ's invitation to "pray ceaselessly" (Lk 18:1), the Rosary allows us to hope that, even today, the difficult "battle" for peace can be won. Far from offering an escape from the problems of the world, the Rosary obliges us to see them with responsible and generous eyes, and obtains for us the strength to face them with the certainty of God's help and the firm intention of bearing witness in every situation to "love, which binds everything together in perfect harmony" (Col 3:14).

The Family: Parents . . .

41. As a prayer for peace, the Rosary is also, and always has been, *a prayer of and for the family*. At one time this prayer was particularly dear to Christian families, and it certainly brought them closer together. It is important not to lose this precious inheritance. We need to return to the practice of family prayer and prayer for families, continuing to use the Rosary.

In my Apostolic Letter *Novo Millennio Ineunte* I encouraged the celebration of the *Liturgy of the Hours* by the lay faithful in the ordinary life of parish communities and Christian groups;[39] I now wish to do the same for the Rosary. These two paths of Christian contemplation are not mutually exclusive; they complement one another. I would therefore ask those who devote themselves to the pastoral care of families to recommend heartily the recitation of the Rosary.

The family that prays together stays together. The Holy Rosary, by age-old tradition, has shown itself particularly effective as a prayer which brings the family together. Individual family members, in turning their eyes towards Jesus, also regain the ability to look one another in the eye, to communicate, to show solidarity, to forgive one another and to see their covenant of love renewed in the Spirit of God.

Many of the problems facing contemporary families, especially in economically developed societies, result from their increasing difficulty in communicating. Families seldom

[39] Cf. no. 34: AAS 93 (2001), 290.

manage to come together, and the rare occasions when they do are often taken up with watching television. To return to the recitation of the family Rosary means filling daily life with very different images, images of the mystery of salvation: the image of the Redeemer, the image of his most Blessed Mother. The family that recites the Rosary together reproduces something of the atmosphere of the household of Nazareth: its members place Jesus at the center, they share his joys and sorrows, they place their needs and their plans in his hands, they draw from him the hope and the strength to go on.

. . . and Children

42. It is also beautiful and fruitful to entrust to this prayer *the growth and development of children*. Does the Rosary not follow the life of Christ, from his conception to his death, and then to his Resurrection and his glory? Parents are finding it ever more difficult to follow the lives of their children as they grow to maturity. In a society of advanced technology, of mass communications and globalization, everything has become hurried, and the cultural distance between generations is growing ever greater. The most diverse messages and the most unpredictable experiences rapidly make their way into the lives of children and adolescents, and parents can become quite anxious about the dangers their children face. At times parents suffer acute disappointment at the failure of their children to resist the seductions of the drug culture, the lure of an unbridled hedonism, the temptation to violence, and the manifold expressions of meaninglessness and despair.

To pray the Rosary *for children*, and even more, *with children*, training them from their earliest years to experience this daily "pause for prayer" with the family, is admittedly not the solution to every problem, but it is a spiritual aid which should not be underestimated. It could be objected that the Rosary seems hardly suited to the taste of children and young people of today. But perhaps the objection is directed to an impoverished method of praying it. Furthermore, without prejudice to the Rosary's basic structure, there is nothing to stop children and young people from praying it—either within the family or in groups—with appropriate symbolic and practical aids to understanding and appreciation. Why not try it? With God's help, a pastoral approach to youth which is positive, impassioned and creative—as shown by the World Youth Days!—is capable of achieving quite remarkable results. If the Rosary is well presented, I am sure that young people will once more surprise adults by the way they make this prayer their own and recite it with the enthusiasm typical of their age group.

The Rosary, a Treasure to Be Rediscovered

43. Dear brothers and sisters! A prayer so easy and yet so rich truly deserves to be rediscovered by the Christian community. Let us do so, especially this year, as a means of confirming the direction outlined in my Apostolic Letter *Novo Millennio Ineunte*, from which the pastoral plans of so many Particular Churches have drawn inspiration as they look to the immediate future.

I turn particularly to you, my dear Brother Bishops, priests and deacons, and to you, pastoral agents in your different ministries: through your own personal experience of the beauty of the Rosary, may you come to promote it with conviction.

I also place my trust in you, theologians: by your sage and rigorous reflection, rooted in the word of God and sensitive to the lived experience of the Christian people, may you help them to discover the biblical foundations, the spiritual riches and the pastoral value of this traditional prayer.

I count on you, consecrated men and women, called in a particular way to contemplate the face of Christ at the school of Mary.

I look to all of you, brothers and sisters of every state of life, to you, Christian families, to you, the sick and elderly, and to you, young people: *confidently take up the Rosary once again*. Rediscover the Rosary in the light of Scripture, in harmony with the Liturgy, and in the context of your daily lives.

May this appeal of mine not go unheard! At the start of the twenty-fifth year of my Pontificate, I entrust this Apostolic Letter to the loving hands of the Virgin Mary, *prostrating myself in spirit before her image in the splendid Shrine built for her by Blessed Bartolo Longo*, the apostle of the Rosary. I willingly make my own the touching words with which he concluded his well-known *Supplication to the Queen of the Holy Rosary*: "O Blessed Rosary of Mary, sweet chain which unites us to God, bond of love which unites us to the angels, tower of salvation against the assaults of Hell, safe port in our universal shipwreck, we will never abandon you. You will be our comfort in the hour of death: yours our final kiss as life ebbs away. And the last word from our lips will be your sweet name, O Queen of the Rosary of Pompei, O dearest Mother, O Refuge of Sinners, O Sovereign Consoler of the Afflicted. May you be everywhere blessed, today and always, on earth and in heaven."

From the Vatican, on the sixteenth day of October in the year 2002, the beginning of the twenty-fifth year of my Pontificate.

JOHN PAUL II